This book is for the forgotten souls, and the endless loves that follow us throughout lifetimes. Also, to my tribe, thank you for doing what you do, and always enjoying the stories that I pour my heart and soul into. Love your faces.

ALSO BY AMELIA HUTCHINS

WICKED HEXES

CURSED COVEN

AMELIA HUTCHINS

WICKED
HEXES

ALSO BY AMELIA HUTCHINS

Upcoming Series

A Crown of Ashes

If you're following the series for the Fae Chronicles, Elite Guards, and Monsters, reading order is as follows:

Fighting Destiny
Taunting Destiny
Escaping Destiny
Seducing Destiny
A Demon's Dark Embrace
Playing with Monsters
Unraveling Destiny
Sleeping with Monsters
Claiming the Dragon King
Oh, Holy Knight
Becoming his Monster
The Winter Court
A Demon's Plaything
If She's Wicked
Embracing Destiny 2019

WARNING!

This book is **dark**. It's **sexy**, hot, and **intensely twisted**. The author is human; you are as well. Is the book perfect? It's as perfect as I could make it. Are there mistakes? Probably, then again, even the **New York Times' top published** books have minimal errors because, like me, they have **human editors**. There are words in this book that won't be found in the **standard dictionary** because they were created to set the stage for a paranormal-urban fantasy world. Words such as 'sift,' 'glamoured' and 'apparate' are common in paranormal books and give better description to the action in the story than can be found in standard dictionaries. They are **intentional** and not mistakes.

About the hero: chances are you may **not** fall instantly in **love** with him, that's because **I don't write men you instantly love**; you grow to love them. I don't believe in **instant-love**. I write flawed, raw, caveman-like **alpha-holes** that eventually let you see their redeeming qualities. They are **aggressive**, **alpha-holes**, one step above a caveman when we meet them. You may **not** even like him by the time you finish this book, but I promise you will **love** him by the **end** of this **series**.

About the heroine: There is a chance that you might think she's a bit naïve or weak, but then again who starts out as a badass? Badasses are a product of growth, and I am going to put her through **hell**, and you get to watch **her** come up **swinging** every time I knock her on her ass. That's just how I do things. How she

Warning! (Cont'd)

reacts to the set of circumstances she is put through, may not be how you as the reader, or I as the author would react to that same situation. Everyone responds differently to circumstances and how Laura responds to her challenges, is how I see her as a character and as a person.

I don't write love stories: I write fast-paced, knock you on your ass, make you sit on the edge of your seat wondering what happens in the next kind of books. If you're looking for cookie-cutter romance, this isn't for you. If you can't handle the ride, ***un-buckle your seatbelt and get out of the roller-coaster car now***. **If not, you've been warned.** If nothing outlined above bothers you, carry on and **enjoy the ride!**

WICKED HEXES

VAMPIRE MATES

CHAPTER ONE

DEEP IN THE LOUISIANA BAYOU
THREE MONTHS BEFORE THE BALL

Braydon

"You understand that if I do this, I will be the villain to her," I snapped, staring at the ancient crone.

"Do you want to save her? Because the only way this ends is with her hating you," she shrugged; her hand cradled the glowing crystal ball that showed me the high mountains of Washington where my mate stared endlessly at the darkening skies. "She won't see it coming. If she suspects it is us summoning her to this celebration, we lose before we ever start to unravel the curse her mother placed on the two of you. She must hate you for a while. Once her transformation has started, you can make her love you again."

"And if she hates me? What then, crone?" I demanded, staring at the glowing quartz sphere that showed me every delicate line of Laura's face.

"Do you love her enough to let her go, my king?" she asked cautiously.

"I've loved her for a thousand years and will love her until I am no more."

"Then make your move, and I will speak to Thea to uphold her end of our bargain. You can handle being her villain until you are once more her prince, Braydon. To save her, you have to destroy her. She may hate you in the end, but to hate you, she must first live long enough to do so."

"Then let it begin, because my pretty little witch is praying to those stars that I never find her. If this doesn't work, if she dies, know that I will follow her into the next life to be with her. She is the moon to my wolf, and without her at my side, the bayou is only a swamp instead of a kingdom." I stared at the witch while her eyes dropped to Laura's. "When what I truly am is revealed, she may never trust me again."

"You're part vampire, part wolf. You're the King of the Hybrids, Braydon. She loved you before, when she thought you were nothing but a washed-up, bitten wolf. She didn't love you for what you were; she loved you for you. Count your stars for that, boy. It's a rare breed of woman who loves a penniless man. Well then, we must begin, shall we?" she smiled, running her fingers over the ball to erase the image.

"I'm ready to hunt my little witch," I admitted. "Let's begin."

CHAPTER ONE

Laura Cheveron

The wind howled gently through the bayou, ruffling my hair. The heat in Louisiana was unbearable, even in October. The scent of late-blooming flowers and sage filled the air. The sound of soft music flowed throughout the mansion, creating a delicate mix of dark and light to match the witches who had gathered for the celebration of Samhain and the promise of an abundant fall harvest.

Inside of the ballroom, couples danced and mingled, reminding me of another time and place long ago, where I'd once done the same with the man I'd loved. Love, it was such a tricky word. It was a flowery word of lies, created by poets of old who sang ballads and sagas of what it was like to experience such a strange emotion. The tale of love was full of lies fed to the heart to make women believe that there was one man out there; one man who would make her heart sing. What those poets and bards forgot to mention was that, by loving someone, you left your hope open, unshielded, and handed your enemies the one thing that could destroy you.

Once upon a time, long, long ago, I'd loved. I'd given Braydon the one thing only I could give him. I'd given him my heart, and by doing so, I'd cursed us to a fate worse than hell. He'd been born mortal, turned werewolf by a curse of fate, and he'd been my enemy. An enemy I'd fallen in love with and dared to dream of a future with.

My mother, learning of my betrayal, cursed us both. Every fifty years, he was reborn to find me, and the moment I fell in love, it turned him berserk, and he went mad with the need to destroy me. One moment he would be my sweet, gentle giant, and the next, he would attack me until it forced me to end his life. Every rebirth, I found him, loved him, and then murdered him to survive. That was also why I'd given up life, living, the so-called daily shit I'd endured to repeat the cycle of the curse she had given us.

My gaze moved to Hope, her ice-blue dress enhancing the sheer beauty of her violet-blue eyes. Ruby-red lips smiled wide, revealing her dimples as suitor after suitor requested to dance with her. Her midnight-colored hair had been twisted into a stylish updo that suited her heart-shaped face perfectly. I'd gone all out on her, pulling in favors from witches and beauticians to give her an entrance into the witch's society befitting our bloodline. Judging from the glares and jealousy floating in the air from the other witches present, it had worked.

My dress was a simple evening dress. The back was held closed with three thin straps, while the front had a deep V-line that exposed the globes of my breasts. The flowing skirt stopped at the ankle, leaving my jeweled sandals exposed. The only jewelry I wore was a thin silver body harness that wrapped around my exposed stomach and latched to the thin, delicate necklace that held a crescent moon in a Celtic pattern, the triple Goddess symbol. I had pulled my hair back, delicate braids twisted into a simple style that left my shoulders naked. It wasn't stylish according to Hope, but it was elegant and allowed my beauty to stand out against the finery we wore tonight for the annual witch's ball.

I lifted the glass of scotch to my lips and inhaled the rich aroma. My eyes wandered the room, passing from Hope and her newest dance partner to the beautiful setting that we stood within. Spanish moss was hanging from the marble pillars that outlined the courtyard. Midnight blue fabric covered the tables, and a spell ignited the air, lighting a glowing orb suspended in the air by magic. Candles had been lit within the sconces, marking the era of the old world for which we'd come. Overall, it was a simplistic beauty that shone with magic.

Magic ignited the surrounding air with power, unavoidable with how many witches were gathered in such a confined space. My naked arms covered in goosebumps as the sense of being watched took root in my center. I surveyed the area, finding nothing out of place. I couldn't shake the feeling of wrongness that seemed to have come out of nowhere.

"She's her mother's daughter, isn't she?" Alyson asked, her crystal blue eyes smiling as she placed a hand on mine and nodded her head. "Don't look so worried, Laura. Not everyone is against the old laws, as Avery assumes. I, for one, have sampled many a vampire within the sheets and don't fault her for her actions. The ancient ways we once followed are just that: archaic and a thing of the past."

"Hope was born both witch and vampire. It makes her a target for those who are living in the past." I wrinkled my nose as James Jameson bowed low at his waist to Hope before trying to cut in on her dance partner.

"Hope has the power of two ancient bloodlines running through her veins. She is both Halverson and Cheveron. Hecate have mercy on anyone who trespasses against that child, because her parents would not give an ounce. Blessed is the girl who survives diversity and can still smile with such innocence. Blessed be, sister," she said with sparkling blue eyes as she moved away from me.

"Blessed be," I muttered, taking another deep drink of the aged scotch.

The foreboding sensation intensified, and I set the glass chalice down and moved toward the ancient Cyprus trees that lined the outer courtyard. My hand fanned my face as I gazed out into the backyard that bordered one of the copses. In the distance, wolves bayed, while other wildlife creatures thrived in the endless swamps of the south. It was one thing I missed about this place; sure, Washington had wildlife running leaps and bounds, but the swamps carried a history with witches that hummed with a life of its own.

"Laura," Kade growled beside me. I turned, smiling at the male who had kept in touch with me through the years, even though I'd thwarted his attempts to date me with my scorned view of love.

"Kade," I nodded, acknowledging his presence. "You look well tonight." He did. He had tied his dark hair behind his neck, and his black suit fit him perfectly, accentuating his broad shoulders and muscular frame.

"You look otherworldly," he said breathlessly, observing me as I turned fully toward him. His dark eyes dipped to my exposed cleavage and then lowered to take in the silver chains that adorned my torso. "I wonder if you'd give me the honor of a dance?" he asked.

"Dancing is for fools; you can offer to buy me a drink."

"Drinks are free," he smirked, tilting his head while watching me. "All the same, I'd enjoy your company while you drank it. Maybe if you get drunk enough, you will forget him tonight, and allow me to cherish you."

"Flirtatious as ever, warlock," I chided, allowing him to claim my hand. His lips touched the back of it before he pulled me with him, directing us toward the benches that faced the open bayou.

We sat facing couples who swayed to the music as the magic wafted through the courtyard, fueled by the endless power of witches who had come from the scattered covens. Once a year, we gathered to celebrate Samhain, to give thanks to the Goddess for the power that ran through our veins.

Traditionally, Samhain was from the old world. A time when the veil between worlds thinned, allowing creatures and spirits in through the Otherworld. We honored those who had come before us, ancestors who, for this one day, could cross the barrier to visit the living. It was also a time when we released old magic and energy to bring new, more powerful magic into our veins.

"Can you sense it as well?" Kade asked, pulling my attention away from the couples to stare into his darkened gaze.

"The unease? Yes," I whispered. "Dark magic is present here. Its intent is unclear to me. I feel it though, oily and slithering through the celebration."

"You are of dark magic, so you among a select few could sense it. Few have been able to dip their toes into it without losing their souls. I envy you that ability, woman."

"Don't be; with it comes an endless need to dip your entire foot into it." I closed my eyes, allowing my senses to seek the dark magic that slipped through the gathering. "Curious, as the sage burns to ward it off," I muttered, opening my eyes, accepting a chalice of scotch and mulled cider from the server who stopped at the table.

"Not as curious as to why you have remained celibate for the last fifty years," he chuckled, pulling my attention from the drinks to his eyes.

"Forty-nine years, and the reasoning is simple. I cannot love, and while I would enjoy scratching the itch, it's pointless for me. I am cursed; I cannot have any pleasure without Braydon. I cannot feel anything without him or his touch. My life is very much black and white, and he the only color I see. You know this, and you deserve someone who can love you, Kade. I am not her. I want that for you as your friend. Besides, why ruin a good thing?" I asked softly, hiding the twisting pain that the memories of Braydon drudged up. "Not to mention, you at least have someone to love, what with having created a life that depends on you."

"Fifty years, my darling," he corrected sadly. "Last time he returned, it was during a leap if I remember correctly, leap year messes up that schedule since it wasn't around when the curse on him was placed."

I stared at him before dropping my gaze. Lifting my eyes, I searched for Hope on the dance floor. Finding her there with yet another young warlock, I turned my attention back to the drink, swallowing hard as the realization staggered me.

"I forgot to account for that," I admitted sheepishly, wondering how that was even possible. I'd always been so careful when the time for him to come back approached. The last time, he'd caught me outside the academy unguarded and unprotected. To protect Avery and the students, I'd gone with him willingly. The time before that, I'd found him and sped up what had to happen so I could prevent our curse from hurting others. "I need to call Avery," I whispered. "Will you excuse me?" At his answering nod, I downed the drink and left the table.

My heart hammered as my gaze swung to the clock, then back to Hope, who danced as if nothing else mattered but the magic that poured through her. Removing my phone from my clutch, I hit call.

"Laura, is everything okay? Is Hope okay?" Avery's panicked tone filled the phone.

"She's fine; her feet, on the other hand, will surely be sore come morning." Avery exhaled once she was sure her daughter was safe. "There's a bigger problem, though. It's something I forgot, and because of it, I need to send Hope home in the morning. She'll be with Kade Mitchell, and…" I paused, staring as Thea, a witch who had been removed from the lines, walked through the crowd with a glowing green aura. "That's strange," I muttered.

"What is strange?" Avery asked, her tone aggravated with not being able to see what was happening.

"Thea is here," I answered, following closely behind the witch that had been denounced because of her use of dark magic in ways unforgivable by the covens.

"Why would she be there? They will never rescind her disownment of magic after what she did."

My eyes swung from Thea as I turned my attention to Hope and noted the distance between them.

"Avery, I need to call you back," I muttered, hissing as something dark slithered over my flesh. My hand moved the phone away from my ear while I swallowed against the pungent scent of dark magic that filled the courtyard. "What the hell?" I whispered, studying Thea, who walked absently to the middle of the crowded room. Everyone in the courtyard stared in curiosity at the dark witch who'd crashed the party.

"What the hell is she doing here?" Kade asked at my side.

"Nothing good," I hissed as the hair on my nape rose in a warning. I started to whisper the incantation of protection as my tongue grew heavy, and the phone dropped from my hand to land upon the concrete floor. "Hope," I cried thickly, my words slurring as Thea spoke.

"'Neath silver moon or dark of night.

In shadow, deep or brightest light.
From this hex none shall be spared.
For wrath knows not peace nor care.
Betrayers! Gather close and hear
I damn you to your darkest fear
I bind you to dread's cold embrace.
Until your truth you boldly face."

My blood turned to ice as Hope's eyes widened in horror, matching mine as the curse splintered through the air, locking every witch into place with the words Thea had growled. Her words seemed to slam through us all as she turned bright green before our eyes. All at once, curses exploded from her, slamming into the witches nearest her before seeking those on the edges of the room. I fell to the floor, crying out as pain gripped my middle, wrenching through me as nausea swirled tightly behind. Everyone present was on their knees, screaming in agony, and when my lips opened to whisper the cure, nothing came out. I closed my eyes against the excruciating pain that split my head in half, throbbing until I wanted to curl into the fetal position and remain there until it had passed. Instead, I swallowed a scream as I tried to get to my feet. My eyes frantically searched for Hope, finding her on the floor with blood streaming from her nose. I could taste my blood as I swallowed, gasping for air as even more pain ripped through me. It took everything I had to get to my feet and start through the twisting bodies of witches who had yet to gain their footing.

"We have to go," I whispered thickly when I reached Hope, pulling her up from the floor. Kade's hand grabbed her other one, helping me lift her from the floor.

"I have no magic," he muttered hesitantly.

"Nor do I," I admitted, albeit embarrassedly. My gaze lingered on the spot Thea had stood, where now only charred marks remained as if she'd exploded with the detonation of the curse. "We're okay," I lied, knowing that whatever had just happened, it was bad, terrible. I was pretty sure we'd just received a death hex, which meant the entire witch community was in serious trouble.

"If we go out the front, and she planned this attack with our enemies, we will be helpless against them," Kade said crossly.

"The bayou," I announced, gazing at him as he picked Hope up in his arms and nodded to me.

We started toward it, ignoring the others who screamed in horror as the realization of being hexed entered their minds. I should have been helping them, and yet I had to keep Hope safe. I'd made a promise to Avery that I'd do everything in my power to keep her daughter safe, and yet I had no power at the moment. I was defenseless.

We'd walked for over thirty minutes, which seemed like an eternity, before I paused, noting our surroundings. We were deep in the bayou, trudging through sludge and thick brush endlessly. I felt eyes on us, and a foreboding sensation trickled up my spine. We weren't alone, and whoever was doing surveillance on us wasn't friendly.

"Kade, stop," I whispered in a hoarse voice. "We're not alone here."

"I'm sorry, Laura. I'm so sorry," he said, turning slowly to set Hope on the ground before he backed away from us.

"What are you talking about?" I asked warily, watching the thick brush around us as wolves seemed to appear from nowhere. No, not wolves; werewolves. "What did you do, Kade?" I demanded in horrified terror.

"They took her, and you were what he wanted to get her back. She's my daughter, Laura. My legacy," he pleaded with his hands out, palms up toward the air as tears slipped from his dark eyes. "He took my daughter. She's my world, and to get her back, all I had to do was deliver you to him. I'm so sorry," he stated, stepping further back as he turned to face the wolf who had transformed into a man. "Where is she? I did what you asked, where's my daughter?"

"She's being walked to the road as we speak," Braydon chuckled, his ice-blue eyes locking with mine before they slipped to my ruined dress. "You have your instructions, Kade, I suggest you follow them. I trust no one noted you leaving the party with my wife?" he asked.

"I did the spell before Thea arrived as you instructed, and unless her hex undid it, no. All they would have seen is Laura helping Hope toward the front entrance where they vanished, and nothing more."

Braydon smiled, triumph shining in his beautiful eyes. Eyes I'd stared into a hundred times before as we'd made love. Eyes I'd watched the life leave upon his death as my magic worked to end it. Now I was his prisoner, and worse, I was defenseless without my magic. Kade started to slip into the brush, and I screamed.

"Take Hope with you; she has no part in this, Kade.

She isn't who he wants!"

"Tsk-tsk, that isn't his choice to make, littlest witch."

"Braydon, please," I begged. "You have me at your mercy, let her go. Her parents will come for her. If you let her go, it will stall them from searching for me."

"You think I care if they come? This is my bayou, my world. Let them come, little one. My wolves enjoy hunting the undead. You once asked me for mercy and then drove your knife through my heart the moment I softened toward you. I won't make that mistake again. You're a traitorous, murderous bitch who enjoys hurting me. It's my turn to hurt you. I promise you, little witch. I have no more mercy within me for you."

"Kade! Take Hope with you," I cried as tears of frustration ran down my face. His shoulders tensed, but Kade didn't stop his forward progress through the thick weeds that he'd walked us into, where he'd ensnared me in Braydon's trap. "I will find you, and I will rip your fucking heart out if you leave her here!" I screamed at his stiffened back. He turned, looking at me one last time before he spoke.

"I know you will, Laura. He had my daughter; she's only seven years old. You're not defenseless. You are a Cheveron, you'll figure it out. You always do."

"Go, Kade, before I let my boys out to hunt early," Braydon snapped while his eyes slid over me with desire banking their wintering depths. "You, sweet girl, come to me," he ordered.

I swallowed, straightening my spine before I glared at him. "You know how this ends, so why rush it?" I asked.

"Not this time, Laura," he said huskily. "This time,

you have no magic, but I do. I'm immortal, and I won't be as easy to kill as I was in the past. Be a good girl, and don't make me into the asshole who threatens to use your sweet little niece against you. Hell, we both know you want me. I'm the only man alive you *can* feel and can make you feel pleasure. Now, do as I say, because we have a long walk home, wife."

"I'm not your wife anymore, Braydon." I stepped forward, lifting the hem of my black dress, which now was beyond saving from the thick Louisiana mud. I closed the distance between us as Hope watched silently. His hand lifted the moment I was close enough to touch, and I flinched, recoiling from what I knew he would make me feel. His ice-blue eyes studied me before he pushed his hand through his long, dark blond hair. His strong jawline sported a neatly trimmed beard, and the thick Viking tattoos he always came back with were present over his sun-kissed skin.

He exhaled and let his fingertips skim over my cheek. My lips parted, and a gasp escaped from my throat while I gaped as molten heat filled his eyes. A cruel smile twisted his lips as he used his other hand to pull me closer to his muscular frame.

Braydon cupped my chin, lifting my face to his as he studied me. "You're even more beautiful than I remember, little one. I will enjoy you fighting this thing between us. You always try to ignore what you feel, and yet you always fail. Come, your new home awaits you."

CHAPTER TWO

Insects buzzed around my head as sweat beaded between my breasts. I was irritable, and yet Hope depended on me keeping her safe, which I would somehow do. Braydon put jeans on while the other wolves had maintained wolf form. Anytime we slowed down, they would nip at our heels to show their displeasure. In the swamp's silence we trudged through, my mind worried what this meant for the innocent young woman who followed behind me. I tripped over a branch I hadn't seen, and Braydon turned, quickly catching me.

"Careful," he said, not letting me go even after I'd righted myself. His thumb raised, tracing over my bottom lip as he regarded me carefully. "Wouldn't want you to get injured, now would we?"

"No, no, why hurt me when you intend to kill me? I mean, logically, it makes total sense, doesn't it?" I snapped irritably, tired of walking through the swamp and in pain from whatever it was Thea had done to me.

"Careful, Laura," he warned as he captured my chin

between his fingers and tilted my mouth to his. "Right now, I'm not sure which I want to do more, kiss you, or shove your sexy little ass off a bridge," he hissed.

"Can I pick?" I countered, staring at his mouth as his lips curved into a sexy smile. Not that I was sure which I would have chosen. Both options held merit, and it had been fifty years since I'd even felt a kiss. Fifty years since I'd felt pleasure or pain.

"And which one, little witch, would you choose?" he demanded, lowering his mouth to hover dangerously close to mine.

"Both," I admitted, moving to claim his mouth, only for him to pull away from me with a mischievous look dancing in his eyes.

"Too bad," he returned, his eyes watching every emotion that played over my face. "There's the fact that your people cursed me, but you cursed me too, so I would remember every fucking life I've lived. What kind of evil bitch would be so cruel?"

"You remember so we can skip to the fun part, Braydon. Would you rather forget me, so that when the madness begins, you're lost and confused about why it is happening? No, hating me, to begin with, is much easier than loving me. I grew tired of falling in love with men, only to find it was you with a different face. I cursed you to remember and to come back to me with the same face, so I would know it was you. I gave you the same memories that I'm cursed to live with, my heart. At least you get death and time to forget the pain. I don't. I have to live knowing I killed the one man who loved me. You want me to pity you? You're not the only one cursed. We both were. Me, for loving you, my sworn enemy, and you for loving me," I swallowed, stepping away from him. "I'm not even a little sorry for leaving you cursed to remember. I loved you enough to leave you a warning of the madness to come. So kill me if that is your wish, put me out of my misery. I fucking dare you, Viking."

"There you are, my foul-mouthed little pagan," he purred. "Don't get my dick hard yet. While I don't mind my pack watching me claim you, I'm sure you don't want an audience. Kade told me you remain chaste when I go away, that's a long time without dick, little witch."

"Didn't Kade tell you? My vow of celibacy wasn't because of you," I smiled coldly. "I decided men weren't worth the trouble. I also stopped caring what they thought of me, which is freeing when you think about it. That also means that you and your penis have no magic over me."

"Are you sure about that?" he asked, grabbing my hand, pulling me forward until it pressed against him. I sensed his hardness stirring and bit down on my tongue to keep the moan trapped where it danced on the tip.

"You, sir, need to calm the hell down. You're at like a twenty, and I need you at a seven," I sputtered, and his lips twitched as he fought a smile.

"What, are you afraid to touch me now? I remember how naughty you are, dirty girl."

"Take my hand off your penis," I whispered huskily as heat pooled between my thighs. "I'm having feelings, and I don't like them."

"No," he smirked wickedly. He was hard, and so were my nipples that chose that moment to stand up as he pressed his body against mine, forcing them to rub against the softness of the dress I wore. "You smell good enough to devour," he chuckled.

"That's not funny."

"I thought it was."

"You don't count, Viking. I'm way too sober for this. I hurt, and you're forcing us to walk through the fucking bayou, so the least you can do is stop making me grab your cock!" I snapped.

His head tipped to the side as he looked down between us where he'd let go of my hand. Yet I continued to hold his cock and stroke it absently. I yanked my hand back and stared at him. Braydon's hand moved to catch me as I started to back away. He chuckled huskily as he nodded to someone behind us, and then silence enveloped the small clearing we stood in.

"Use the pond to wash the blood from your face," he instructed.

My hand rose and found blood crusted on my nose. My head was heavy as if it was being cleaved in two by a giant battle ax instead of a hex. I eyed him suspiciously before turning to look at the murky water. I didn't wait for an invitation; I made my way to the small creek and knelt in front of it, cupping the water before I washed my face off. The cool water was bliss against the aching of my face.

I remained there longer than needed, enjoying the respite from roaming through the bayou. Eventually, I got up and turned around and then noted what I had missed. Hope had vanished, and it left me alone with Braydon.

"Where is she?" I demanded as panic surged through

me.

"Right now, she's behind a locked door," he shrugged, crossing his muscular arms over his naked chest. "She's safe for the time being. How long that remains the case, well, that depends on you."

"Do it," I breathed, closing my eyes. "Just get on with it."

I tipped my head back, praying to the Goddess that this man, the only man I'd ever trusted with my heart, hurried my death and made it as painless as I'd tried to make his. I was prepared for his hands around my neck, for his knife to pierce my heart, but not his mouth to brush against mine. His large hands encircled my waist, holding me in place as a moan slipped from my throat. The heat of his lips sent a storm raging through me.

"I dream of you, every fucking night. I see you from the moment I close my eyes until I open them in the morning. You haunt me, witch. You cursed me to a hell of unimaginable agony. No woman satisfies my hunger, nor even whets my appetite."

"That sounds more like a *you* problem," I returned, pushing him away from me. His eyes burned with a hunger I knew well. He smiled, but it was anything but friendly. "You should just end it now. Quick and easy, because then you can live, Braydon. I am the only thing keeping you cursed. My death is your freedom."

"I'm fully aware of what your death will do to me. You seem to forget the biggest fucking problem with me remembering. I remember loving you."

"Here's the thing, Braydon, it isn't my problem." I wanted him pissed. I wanted this over with so he would free Hope to go home and live a normal life.

She deserved it, and I knew this only ended with one of us dead. It was a curse and a powerful one at that. She couldn't be here when his madness kicked in, or when his sanity fled, and he turned on me. Every time he'd ever captured me, I'd had one defense against him, magic. Thea had taken my magic somehow. I was one hundred percent fucked without it. We both knew it.

"No, it isn't. Your problem is this," he said, closing the distance between us. "You're my prisoner, and you have no magic. You have no way to escape me this time."

"I don't want to escape you," I replied, noting the narrowing of his eyes at my reply. "Do you remember what I said as you died from poison in your last rebirth?" I asked.

"That it would be the last time you took my life." He snorted as a sardonic smile tilted his mouth. "You failed, because here I am, sweet girl."

"I didn't fail, Braydon. It wasn't your death that triggers the end of this curse. It's mine. Maybe this was the Goddess's way of forcing my choice. Witches are ingrained with the need to survive. To live until the coven comes to save you. Our magic guides them to us. It protects us until they can reach us. So, I didn't fail." I smiled sadly as I watched his smile fade. "When the madness takes you, you will murder me, and you will end the curse. I will not murder you, so this cycle will be the last dance we share. The world cursed us to be soulmates. My mother cursed us to find one another in every rebirth and to fall in love all over again. Once we hit that mark, it triggers your madness. The curse that unleashes your berserker to destroy me, and how you do destroy me is beautifully poetic. I'm the battle you wage, and the one you never win. Until now, now you have me defenseless, and you will kill me."

"You think I haven't taken precautions against that happening? You're not the only witch in the bayou or the only one who wants this to end differently. Curses have an out clause, witch. You know that. You never even bothered looking for it."

"I searched the fucking world for it, Braydon! I scoured this world endlessly as I avoided you to prevent the inevitable from happening. On your first rebirth, I avoided you like the black plague that visited London. I sought cures in new worlds and old ones. I sought voodoo priestesses and monsters alike to save you from me. The only thing that freed you from it was playing out. So do whatever it is you plan to do to me. I'm exhausted. My magic is gone, and I feel as if I've been torn into pieces and scattered throughout the realms. I need to rest, please."

"You want mercy from me?" he snorted, his eyes slowly taking in my stained dress and the slump of my shoulders.

"You need to hurry with the three F's, Viking." My hand lifted, running against the side of my temple, where a new pounding had begun.

"The three F's?" he inquired carefully, his eyebrows pinched together in question.

"Free me, fuck me, or feed me. I don't care which order you proceed in, but you need to do one of them soon," I mumbled thickly as a popping noise sounded in my head. My nose exploded, and blood dripped down my chest as I swayed on my feet.

"Little witch," he murmured before he caught me as I began to pass out. I sensed his strong, warm embrace as he lifted my body in his arms, cradling me closely against his. "I have you, Laura," he whispered against my ear as I gave in to the blackness that pulled me down.

CHAPTER THREE

The smell of a male brought me awake from a dead sleep. Arms had wrapped around me, and I pressed my body against the hard muscles that offered protection. The fact that his flesh touched mine told me he'd removed our clothes before placing me into his bed. In sleep, Braydon was masculinity in raw perfection. High chiseled cheekbones cut strikingly against his bronzed cheeks, dusted by thick, black lashes. His full lips brought up sinful memories of what they'd done to my body, time after time. His beard was full and yet trimmed. Sleep had tousled his dark, blond hair. Absently, I lifted a hand to push the stray strands away from his face.

I yelped as his hand caught mine before I touched him. His massive body rolled mine, trapping me beneath him as his large hand captured my wrist high above my head, holding me with his weight alone. Ice-blue eyes, the same color of the fjords of Norway in winter, watched me through half-hooded slits.

"Careful, little witch," he warned, lowering his

mouth to kiss the hammering pulse in the hollow of my throat. His hips ground against mine, the erection sending my need to a boiling burn that threatened to undo me.

"Or what?" I whispered, inhaling his unique scent that was a drug through my system. My hips rolled invitingly, knowing that I was in a precarious position, but it didn't matter. Nothing ever had when I was with him.

He chuckled darkly as he allowed me to grind against his silken length until my arousal glistened over it. My nipples pebbled with the need for him to touch them, and everything woman in me screamed for the berserker to let loose. I moaned as his cock skimmed over the ball of nerves in my clitoris as he growled hungrily, watching every emotion that played over my face.

"You're playing with fire, one that you won't survive if lit, woman." His warning trembled through me, and I blinked past the tears that pricked my eyes.

I bucked against him, twisting my arms as my eyes closed, blocking the fire banked in his blue eyes. "Get off of me, Neanderthal," I whispered, praying he released me before he heard the rapid tempo of my heart, which beat for him and him alone.

"What's the matter, little girl? Afraid to let that pretty pussy get eaten by the big bad wolf?" he uttered hoarsely.

"Let me go, Braydon," I demanded through the tightness of my lips.

He released me, and I turned away as he rolled to the edge of the bed gracefully, standing up. I gripped the thin material of the sheet tightly, staring at his naked form. I struggled to calm my body's reaction to his, and the memories of what that body made me feel. I needed to keep my focus sharp if I had any chance of getting Hope out of this mess alive.

"You need to release Hope Halverson, Braydon. You have me; she has no part in this." I swallowed as he turned around, uncaring that his heavy cock hung freely from the dark blonde curls that cradled it. I averted my stare, taking in the ancient runes carved into the wall of his bedroom.

"No," he said coldly. "Not until I remove the mark you placed on my soul, and then you both will be free to leave here."

"What?" I asked, swinging my gaze to his. "I didn't mark you, Braydon. You're my soulmate. That wasn't something I asked for or had any more control over than you did. If it could have been removed, I would have."

"Not by your people it can't," he snorted as he slipped on gray sweatpants while he continued to stare at me. "Do you think I didn't plan your capture, witch? I'm not the naïve Viking who fell for your pretty green eyes anymore. You're here so that this ends. Your mark on my soul will be removed, and you will leave here the moment I achieve that goal."

"Are you mad already? There is no way to remove a mark from the soul! Don't you think I considered that? I thought maybe if it wasn't upon our souls, you wouldn't love me, and the curse would never trigger. It was the first thing I tried, and everywhere I went, everyone I spoke to said the same fucking thing. We cannot remove it. It is a rare marking of souls that follows those who hold it through every lifetime they live."

"You never came to New Orleans then, because there's older magic than yours here. I will remove your mark, so I don't want or crave you. Your magic forced this marking on me, not something else. You did this to me! I can't fuck another woman without seeing your face and wishing it was you I savaged. I can't love the mate I have chosen because of you!"

I recoiled as if he'd slapped me with his words. My stomach dropped to the floor before bouncing up into my throat. My heart hammered against my chest as hot tears pricked my eyes.

"You're mated?" I whispered.

"I will be soon enough," he said coldly. "Once you're gone from my system."

In all the time since I'd met Braydon, I'd never known him to take another lover after the mark had begun craving my soul. It was why I'd taken no one else intimately but him since the first time I'd laid with him, knowing no other man alive could come close to what he made me feel. I tightened my hold on the sheet until my knuckles turned white.

"Where are my clothes?" I demanded crossly, scanning the room for them. A shirt hit the side of my face, and I followed it with my eyes as it fell to the floor. "I'm not wearing your clothes, Viking. Where are mine?"

"I don't think you understand your position here, Laura," he chuckled wickedly. "You're my prisoner, and you will wear what I say you will wear. Your dress is in ruins, and we disabled the spells on your chains. I have them someplace safe, woman."

"Those chains belonged to my mother," I snapped.

"A mother who cursed her own daughter to a fate worse than hell," he sneered. "You have two choices, you can wear my shirt, or you can wear my sheets. I don't fucking care which one you choose. Do not leave this room, do you understand me, witch?" he asked.

"Or what?" I countered.

"Or I'll spank your pretty ass until it aches," he returned, dropping his eyes to the sheet I held to shield my nudity. "Who knows, you may even like it. You were always such a dirty little girl before, weren't you, little one?"

"Try me, fucker, and you will wish you had never met me."

"Too late, I already wish I'd never laid eyes on you, woman," he snapped as he opened the door and slammed it in my face, leaving me numb.

Every time Braydon returned, he'd been gentle, loving, and much akin to the man they had sent me out to assassinate. I dropped the sheet and picked up the shirt, holding it up before I slipped it on and then sniffed it. Nordic winters clung to the shirt, and the promise of ice and snow mixed with the man who owned it filled my nose. I slipped it back off, folding it gently before I set it back on the bed and retrieved the sheet, wrapping it around me like the finest dress.

The room mirrored a different era, with no windows or light from outside. Candles sat upon the chest of drawers that lined the wall. I moved, retrieving the matches to light a single flame before I studied the walls. One door led out of the room, and he'd warned me not to open it, and yet my bladder was making my needs known. There was also the fact that I'd pecked at food yesterday and hardly eaten before the ball.

My fingers traced the runes before I made my way to the single chair that adorned the room and sat down in it, placing the candle onto the small table beside it. I rested my head against the back and considered my options.

I had to get outside of this room to see where Hope was being held. I needed to learn their defenses, and find out if they had men guarding her. Without magic, it would be tricky to get to her, but I would do whatever it took to free her of this place. I owed it to Avery to keep her daughter safe, and I'd failed miserably. And now she was being held by a man who was a ticking time bomb. One that would activate the moment I started to fall in love with him. He'd be unable to stop himself, cursed to become the berserker who savaged me until he ended my life. My life had been lived fully, but not Hope's. She'd just barely experienced this world and what it could offer her. I wasn't afraid of dying; dying was only a new chapter in a new world, and I was ready. Braydon deserved to be happy and live his life without paying for my sins.

CHAPTER FOUR

Hours had passed without Braydon returning. Hours that I'd waited, ignoring my body's need until it was too much to ignore. I knocked on the door, waited for someone to answer, and when that didn't happen, I twisted the knob, and the door opened into a larger room. I stepped through the doorway with the sheet wrapped firmly around me. Gradually, I moved out of the bedroom, but a deep growl stopped me in my tracks. I turned slowly, finding a large gray wolf baring its sharp teeth at me.

"Good doggie," I said carefully. "I'm only looking for the bathroom."

It snarled and started toward me, forcing me back into the room where I slammed the door closed. I leaned against it and groaned. This was torture. I was still holding onto the knob with my back against it when the door pushed open, sending me onto the floor with the sudden burst of speed in which he used to open it.

"I warned you," he snapped.

"I have to pee!" I snapped back, lifting my sore body

from the floor as he watched me through narrowed eyes. "You left me in here all day, and I haven't peed since yesterday! I don't know how wolves do it, but I didn't think you wanted me pissing around your room!"

He folded his arms over his chest and glared at me as if I was lying. My knees crossed as I groaned. Braydon snorted before turning to show me the way. I followed him, ignoring the huge wolf that watched my every move. He opened a door and stepped aside as I rushed into the room, slamming the door in his face before I ran for the toilet. I groaned in bliss as I emptied my overly full bladder. Once I'd finished, I turned to stare out the window before flushing. Swamp filled every inch of visible land outside the bathroom. Were we away from the others? Didn't wolves stick together and live in one large house? I turned back to stare at the door, fixing the sheet over my body when Braydon opened the door, leaning against the wall as his eyes slid down the length of me.

"Get out," I growled, adjusting the sheet once more before turning to flush the toilet.

"It's my bathroom," he stated.

"Well then, let me go, and I'll gladly use my own," I offered angrily.

"Soon," he returned.

"I'm hungry," I said, changing the subject.

"Not my problem." His eyes danced with mirth as he watched me struggling with the sheet.

I shook my head before I marched out of the bathroom and back into the bedroom. I moved to the chair, preferring it to the bed which smelled of him. I brought my legs up and wrapped my arms around them, ignoring my stomach, which waited until he stormed into the room before it let loose a loud complaint from lack of food.

"Pouting?" he asked.

"No, I'm praying for death. Something you seem incapable of delivering, pussy!" I hissed.

Braydon picked me up from the chair and tossed me onto the bed. He grabbed the sheet, taking it from me as my body rolled out. I turned to attack, only for him to slam me against the mattress and grab a fistful of my hair as his teeth skimmed my shoulder, and his hand landed hard against my ass. I yelped and bucked against him, trying to dislodge his hand from my hair, which he used to hold me down.

His hand repeatedly landed against me, burning the flesh of my ass as I screamed in outrage. My anger rose, and I reached for my magic to attack him, only to grasp emptiness. The sense of hopelessness washed through me. I was defenseless, and the one thing I'd always counted on to protect me wasn't there anymore. Tears fell unchecked as he continued to assault my ass with his bare hand, and then it changed. He rubbed the aching flesh as I buried my head in the mattress, silently taking what he gave.

His lips pressed against the sore flesh of my shoulder where his teeth had drawn blood, and he released my hair. Braydon's knees parted my legs, and I tensed as his finger slipped between them.

"Stop," I whispered brokenly as he paused at my entrance.

"You don't want me to stop."

"But I do," I returned, waiting for him to take what

he wanted. He didn't. Instead, he pulled away from me, rising from the bed to stare down at what he'd done to my ass. My cheeks burned with the embarrassment of it, but worse, the wetness that stood glistening between my now parted legs. I closed them, pulling the sheet over my body as I curled into a ball and stared at the wall.

I remained there until the door closed, showing his exit. Tears slipped free the moment it closed, and I lifted from the bed, moving back to the chair, wincing with every step I took. My ass was on fire, but it had hurt my pride more than anything else. I hadn't been defenseless since I'd been a mere child in the late 1200s. It was a foreign feeling, but grasping for my magic and discovering a void within me where it had always been, it had driven home the helplessness of my position.

The door opened, and I turned, staring at a woman. She was beautiful, with long blonde hair braided down her back. Blue eyes surveyed me harshly before she entered the room, her ample breasts visible through the thin dress she wore. I didn't blame her for her wardrobe, not when even in October, this place was hot as hell. Louisiana never got the message that winter was upon it, nor did it seem to care.

She set a platter of meat, cheese, and bread down on the small table before turning to study me.

"You are smaller than I thought you would be," she mused. "You don't look evil." I studied her carefully, noting the intensity of her stare and the delicate bone structure of her face. She was a werewolf, and if I had to pick a rank, it was a beta more than an omega. "You could just free him of your curse. He doesn't deserve this, no one does."

"No, he doesn't deserve it. If I could undo it, I'd have done it the moment my mother cursed him. He seems to forget the part where I am cursed too. Not that it is any of your concern," I snapped irritably. Just who the hell did she think she was?

"I will mate with him. I don't care that he sees you when we fuck. I will do anything and everything needed for me to protect my pack."

My stare narrowed as I snorted. "Good, good for you," I offered, mostly because I couldn't find anything else to say.

"I could just kill you now," she offered pointedly.

"You could, but the curse only ends when he takes my life. If anyone else intervenes, we are reborn to repeat it within days of our death. If I kill him, in fifty years, he will find me, and we will repeat this cycle," I shrugged as if it didn't matter. "It is a curse on our souls. You kill me, and he won't forget me. It won't free him, because he will then become the hunter. But by all means, put me out of my fucking misery."

"Why curse him in the first place?" she asked, sitting on the bed.

"I didn't," I offered in reply before swallowing hard against the memories. "My mother sent me to kill him, but what I found wasn't a monster. Braydon was supposed to be a murderous beast, but that wasn't what I found. Instead, I found this warrior tending to sick children who most likely would have drowned to end their suffering. He challenged me, and I found it cute that he thought he stood a chance. Eventually, we fucked and fell in love with one another. My mother discovered my treachery, and she cursed me to murder the only man I have ever loved. Fifty years later, he came back to me, but madness overtook him. He became the monster they said he was, and it forced me to kill him to survive. Braydon is berserker, and when the madness takes him, it is my body he savages. My lesson from my mother that my soulmate was the monster she warned me about. He can't help it any more than I can. He is the only one who can end this. When he ends my life, he will be free of me."

"Then why haven't you let him kill you before now?" she questioned.

"I am a witch, and everything within me demands I stay alive to keep my bloodline thriving. My magic doesn't allow me to give in easily. I have been cursed with immortality. That means he and he alone can end my life. He is the only weapon on this earth that can end my existence. Don't worry your pretty little head, blondie. I fully intend for him to end this," I laughed coldly.

"Enough talking," Braydon snapped from the doorway where he'd been listening to the conversation. "Moira, my darling, you're finished in here. Josie needs help with the elderly. Go tend to them with her."

I watched as her gaze swung to his, filling with a deep tenderness that his didn't match. Wolves didn't mate for love; they did it to breed and for protection of the pack or to ally with another pack. She, however, was positively besotted by Braydon, not that I blamed her. I tore my gaze from them and faced the wall, ignoring the food as my stomach churned with unease and jealousy. It was selfish to want him to only want me, but it didn't change that while he may have been reborn without the love I felt, I never escaped it.

He closed the door, sealing me into the room, and I closed my eyes as I whispered a spell to extinguish the candle and protect Hope through the night, opening them again when I realized nothing had happened. I stood and leaned over, blowing out the candle before settling back into the chair. I winced as my sore backside hit the cushion. Asshole. I should have looked for a weapon to leave my mark on him, and yet exhaustion made me weak. My eyes closed as my mind wandered freely through the memories of another time and place where he'd loved me and not her.

CHAPTER FIVE

Someone lifted me without warning. I squirmed to get free, fighting against the hold until arms tightened against me. The smell of alcohol hit me before the scent of male did. I stilled, turning toward his woodsy aroma, and he chuckled huskily. I looked down at my chest, noting the room was dark, making it hard to see, but if I had to guess, I'd say he left my sheet on the chair purposely.

"I can walk, puppy," I murmured irritably at the disturbance to my sleep.

"You were sleeping in a chair," he said, dropping me onto the bed. I bounced hard, landing on the floor in a crumpled heap, crying out in shock. "Fucking hell, I thought you weighed more than that, woman."

"What the hell is your issue with tossing me around?" I grumbled, sitting up, growling as he once again lifted me and sat on the bed with me cradled in his arms.

"You have eaten nothing, my wicked little witch."

"Not yours, Viking. Now let me go," I whispered, hating the emotion that flared through me with his endearment. "I'm sure your mate will warm your bed, but I will not. You're drunk, and I'm exhausted."

"She isn't my mate, yet," he shrugged, which jostled me in his lap. "I wouldn't curse her with what you did to me. She deserves a man who sees her and not another woman's face as he takes her. I only see you and crave your cunt when I fuck others."

"You think I care who you see when you come? At least you *can* come! I don't get sex without you; my cunt doesn't work without you! I'm *so* sorry it is my face you see when you fuck, but it could be worse. I can't even get myself off, so your problem seems pretty fucking lame in comparison!" I struggled to get out of his arms, hating his hold as I'd blurted the truth to him.

He chuckled huskily, allowing me to stand up. I turned, looking through the darkened room as my eyes adjusted. The moment I could move without stumbling in the dark, I did. I was almost back to the chair when I sensed him behind me. I slowly turned, continuing my trek backward until something cold touched my back. I searched the darkness, only finding him when his hands landed on the wall, trapping me between them.

His mouth lowered, hovering over mine as my chest rose and fell with both fear and excitement. The moment his hands dropped, and he stepped back, I exhaled. He stared through the darkness, having me at a huge disadvantage without my magic. I leaned my head back, closing my eyes against the hormones and need that rushed through me. I could scent it better than most. The arousal coated my sex, the need to be destroyed by the one man who could do it. I dropped my head against the wall, opening my eyes as the touch of his hand cupping my breast stilled me. I gasped as his roughened thumb traced over the puckered bud before his mouth crushed against mine.

He demanded entrance, pushing his tongue past my lips as his hands abandoned my breasts to grip my chin, holding me there for his hungry mouth. The other hand slipped to my lower back, pulling me against him as we dueled for dominance of the kiss. He sucked my tongue, nipping it before he pulled back, dropping to his knees. My hands found his shoulders, grabbing them as I struggled to pull him back up to my mouth, where I needed him. He chuckled wickedly before his lips clasped against my clit and I cried out as shock raced through me.

Braydon flicked it enticingly with his tongue, playing with my sex as his fingers pushed through my flesh, entering my body slowly. He growled, the sound vibrating through my clit as he released it, peering up through the darkness as I held on to him so I wouldn't crumble from what he did. My knees weakened, threatening to deposit me upon the floor. Another finger entered me, and I screamed at the fullness it created as the orgasm danced just out of reach. My body moved against him as he watched me, fighting to reach the height that only he could bring me to, but the moment I started to unravel, he withdrew from my body. I opened my mouth to beg him to finish, but his cold laughter stopped the plea from leaving my lips. He stood up, pushing his fingers into his mouth as I watched him.

"You're fucking delicious," he growled before he turned, giving me his back as he pulled off his shirt and discarded it onto the floor.

I watched him in silence as he stripped naked and then started toward the bed without paying me any heed. Exhaling slowly, I fought my need to plead with him for the release that had been within grasp, only for him to stop. I slid into the chair, pulling the sheet over me, closing my eyes, ignoring the virile male that had just slurped his fingers clean of my arousal.

"Get your ass into this bed," he ordered.

"Fuck you." I snarled in frustration.

"It wasn't a request. Keep in mind, I hold your niece, and I'm not the Viking who saved children on that shore so long ago. Your problem is this; you assume I am the same man. I'm not. You and your curses fucked me. They made me into someone who can be led around blindly by you and your tight pussy. I found a witch of my own before coming for you last time. I'm not the man you loved, not entirely. The runes on my body, they're mine this time, not yours. Laura, get your sweet tasting cunt into this bed, so I don't do something you'll regret later."

I stood unwillingly and slowly moved to the bed, crawling onto it as he inspected me through hooded eyes. His smile wasn't friendly, more like a predator stalking its meal as it walked into a well-planned trap. My small breasts caught his gaze, and he watched them as I settled on the bed, glaring at him with unease. Ignoring him, I closed my eyes and pretended to sleep. His hand landed on my hip, and I jolted, opening my eyes wide as he slowly explored my curves with his fingertips.

"You're too skinny," he grumbled. "Fucking tiny, all of you is tiny."

"Sorry to disappoint you," I muttered crossly. "Go fuck Moira; she has ample curves and assets."

"You sound jealous," he whispered huskily. I didn't respond as my skin rose with the awareness of his slow, leisure examination. He let the tips of his fingers test the globe of my breast, pinching the nipple without warning, which pulled a moan from my lips.

"Do you mind?" I watched him carefully, noting that he didn't bother even looking at me before he responded to my question.

"No, I don't. You can touch me if you want to. I will let you molest me," he murmured, lifting his eyes to lock with mine. He smirked, leaning over to suck one raised peak into his heated mouth. His eyes never left mine as he scraped his teeth over the sensitive flesh. My eyes grew heavy with lust and started to shut, but he bit down harder, stealing a cry from my lungs as pain mingled with pleasure. "Keep your fucking eyes open, little witch."

"This is torture," I hissed, arching into his mouth as he sucked against the swollen tip greedily. He laughed around the mouthful he held, and his other hand slipped between my thighs, parting them until they dropped open as he pushed me onto my back, leaning up to look at the swollen flesh of my sex.

"Fifty years and nothing has touched this pretty slit? You didn't even try to get off, did you?" he questioned.

"What would be the point? I can't get aroused without you. I feel nothing, and my body responds only to you, not me, and no other man."

"How many men have known you in this way?" he asked.

"Two," I replied. "You and the lover I took when you had been gone forty-nine years, and I had one left before you were to be reborn." His hand paused, tearing his eyes from my swollen flesh to glare into mine. "I allowed a lover to take the blood of my virginity to end the curse before I'd found you again. It didn't work."

"You whored yourself out to protect me?" he snapped.

A blush of embarrassment flooded my cheeks. I closed my legs against his damnation of my action. I'd made a deal with a warlock, one who assured me he could break the curse and protect Braydon from it. I'd have sold my soul to protect him from being ensnared in my mother's curse, and yet he damned me for it.

"There was nothing I wouldn't do to protect you." I pushed him away, sitting up to give him my back. "You can think the worst of me if it helps you sleep at night, Braydon. It matters little to me," I uttered.

His hand pushed the hair away from my neck as his lips touched against it. I shivered from the pure intimacy of the act. His heated kiss sent butterflies into flight in my belly as he pulled me back against the heat of his body. The room filled with shadows as his fingers slipped down my naked stomach to skim over my cunt. I gasped as he moved them through the wetness of my apex, creating a storm of sensation that brought unshed tears to my eyes.

"You want this," he growled against my shoulder before his teeth skimmed the flesh. His other hand lifted to my throat, holding me prisoner with the light touch alone. "How easy it would be to make you mine, littlest witch," he murmured. A single digit pushed into my body as a moan escaped past my lips. "It's a shame that I don't like you because my body doesn't seem to care that you're my enemy."

"Would you rape me, Viking? Pillage me as you did the innocent maidens of your enemies? If so, do it. My body may crave you, and my soul may weep for your touch, but my mind fucking hates you." I shivered as he pushed another finger into my body, stretching it as his grip tightened against my throat. He laughed darkly, sucking against the pulse that danced in a steady beat as my body responded to what he did to me.

"I wouldn't need to rape you, wife. You are mine. The curse you placed on me allowed me to remember what you feel like as you come undone on my cock. The way your eyes grow heavy as my name escapes your pretty pink fuckable lips while you come on my cock. You made it so, and the only reason I can think of so I crave you and only you. I remember the tightness of this flesh, the heat of it wrapped around me so lovingly. I know what you like and what drives you over the edge. I also know that you're a cold bitch who enjoys pain," he said huskily as he withdrew his fingers to the knuckles and slowly pushed them in deeper. "I know you, and everything you like, and how being manhandled turns you on, and enjoy when I become rough with you. You beg when I fucking destroy this pretty cunt, demanding I fuck this naughty slit until it is swollen from what you crave. Tell me how to undo this curse, and I'll make you come for me, pretty girl," he offered gutturally.

"Kill me," I replied. "Kill me, and it ends."

"No," he snapped as his fingers withdrew and rubbed over the swollen nub of my sex. "I won't let you make me into a monster like you are. I want to know what magic will end this, and how to ensure that I am through with you and your kind."

"There is no magic that will undo the mark on your soul, nor mine. I'm sorry for loving you and forcing you into this curse, but once upon a time, Braydon, you loved me too. I warned you that my love came with a cost, and you told me you would pay it to be my husband. You took me to the chapel, and before our gods, we were married. We knew my mother would find out, and you didn't care as long as I became yours in every way a woman can belong to a man. She did, and she cursed us to this fate together."

"I'm not the same man who loved you, witch. I am the monster who craves your cunt and nothing else. I don't remember agreeing to be your husband, and yet I can feel that you are mine and my wife. I loathe you and your kind, selfish bitches who care not about others as long as you get what you want. I know you because I remember you, but you mean less than nothing to me."

I swallowed as silent tears ran down my face in the darkened room. His grip tightened on my throat, stealing the air to my lungs as his fingers pinched the delicate ball of nerves. I didn't move or respond to the pain that threatened to escape from my lungs. His teeth nipped the hollow column of my throat, and I did nothing. He chuckled ominously, releasing his hold on my clit, and rubbed his knuckles through the mess of my cunt as stars burst into my vision. My lungs ached to get air, and yet I didn't fight him. I didn't respond.

"No sweet noises for me, bitch?" he asked roughly. His knuckles paused as his fingertips slipped through the folds, pushing into my body, and it took everything within me to hold the moan at bay. The coppery taste of my blood hit my tongue while I held the moan trapped in my throat. He moved deeper, working them to a steady beat that brought me to the edge of release. His hand loosened on my throat, and yet I still made no noise.

"Release me," I whispered weakly through trembling lips.

"Never," he promised.

I gasped as he pushed another finger into my body, stretching it until it burned with pain from years of neglect. He threaded his other hand through my hair, pulling my head back until his heated breath fanned my ear. He laughed coldly, using it to stand me up before he bent me over, using his feet to push my legs apart.

"Messy girl, this dirty cunt is weeping to be fucked, isn't it?" he asked hoarsely. He held control, and he knew it, yet he slowly continued to stretch me, something he'd done often before considering the thickness of his sex. He was too big, and I too small. I was delicate compared to his height of well over six feet, compared to my tiny five feet and one inch.

I was close to unraveling, and yet I fought it. I wouldn't let him do what he wanted, which was to force the orgasm from me. He wanted to punish me for what he thought I had done to him, fine. But this, this wasn't something he could do to me. I wouldn't let him make the one thing we did so well together be ugly. When my body didn't cave to his demands, he ripped me up by my hair, turning me to look into his eyes. He flinched when he found my eyes wet with tears. My chest heaved with anger as he watched me, holding my hair painfully twisted in his fist.

"Your tears won't save you, little girl," he warned with a roughness in his tone that sent a ripple of longing through my body.

"I didn't think they would. Rape me if you must, Viking. Take what you want and then let me sleep."

"I'm only marking you," he growled raspingly. "Can't have your unclaimed cunt luring my men to it," he threw me toward the bed, where I cried out as I turned over, watching him stroke his thick cock. "I won't have my men touching your flesh when it lures them to their deaths. Part your legs and hold still for me, woman. Fight me, and I'll fuck you so hard you won't be able to move for days from the pain."

I watched him as he crawled onto the bed, settling between my legs, where he pushed them apart painfully. I closed my eyes tightly against the sight of his magnificent body. The sound of his hand slipping over his delicate flesh forced my eyes back open with curiosity. In all of our time together, he'd never done this before. His icy stare locked with my curious gaze. He continued slowly working his cock, which he'd aimed at my sex. Braydon didn't touch me as he started pumping himself harder. The muscles in his chest tightened with strain, and the muscles in his throat flexed tightly. He hissed, and hot juts of his come covered my apex as I stared at it. His hand moved, rubbing his come over my flesh in slow, measured strokes that created arousal within me. My eyes closed as my lips parted, ignoring him as he worked his scent into my flesh to mark me off-limits to his men.

He continued rubbing, grazing my clitoris until my

breathing grew labored while he watched me, knowing he was holding me teetering on the edge of the storm. The moment my body inched toward the cliff, he stopped.

"Do you want me to finish it?" he asked softly with no hate marring his tone.

"No," I whispered, scooting away from him until I was on the edge of the bed. I stood on trembling legs and grabbed the sheet with shaky hands, wrapping it around me before I sat down.

"I can help you, Laura," he offered. "Tell me how much you need me, and I will help you out."

"Go to hell, Braydon."

"I'm already there, little one," he muttered. "The only difference between this time and the last one is that I intend to put you through hell with me."

CHAPTER SIX

I woke to an empty room filled with his scent clinging to everything within it, even me. I stood and stretched my aching limbs, eyeing the bed longingly, and yet the pile of folded clothes on the bed caught my attention. I dropped the sheet and winced at the tender flesh between my thighs. It was red, but then so was my ass where he'd slapped it the night before. Holding up the sheer dress that did little to hide anything, I slipped it on and then gazed into the mirror that had been placed in the room while I slept.

Glaring at my wild hair and the matching dark circles around my eyes, I let my gaze slip to the sheer material of the dress. I could see the pink tips of my nipples, along with the red patch of hair that marked the apex of my sex. I turned slowly, discovering a brush and hairbands that had been set on the dresser. Moving to them, I grabbed the brush and slowly worked it through my hair until it was smooth. It took over an hour to make the three separate war braids before I wrapped them together in the way Braydon had always preferred

I wear my hair.

Moving the chair, I picked up the discarded sheet and folded it, placing it back onto the bed before I took my position in the chair. The door opened, and Braydon walked into the room, covered in dirt and sweat. My gaze lingered on his before I dismissed him. I heard his deep inhale before it whistled out as he walked toward me, kneeling between my legs as he held them apart and inhaled while I gazed down at him.

"Afraid to come outside?" he challenged as he stood slowly, crossing his arms over his chest, studying me. "Or are you hoping for me to ravish you?"

"You told not to leave this room, and the thought of your hands touching me again seems to induce vomit to rise in the back of my throat. I'm willing to stay put like the good little whore you want me to be, puppy."

"Whore?" he asked, hiking one dark brow toward his forehead with the question.

"Isn't that what you called me last night? Or was it evil, vile witch whose pussy was poisonous? I'm sure you can pick which name you want to call me today. Try changing it up a bit to keep me wondering which offensive thing you'll use," I offered with a shrug as my stomach growled.

"You need to eat, woman. You're too tiny as it is, losing weight will make it worse."

"Don't bother yourself, I'm immortal," I muttered. "I want to see Hope now."

"Too fucking bad," he chuckled, sitting on the bed to stare me down. "Stand up, woman."

"No," I said obtusely, glaring at him. He stood fluidly, plucking me from the chair by my arms. My chest rose and fell in anger as I stared murderously up at him.

"Turn around and let me see your pretty ass, witch," he spat out as if I was something vile. I turned, allowing him to see the red welts along with the bruises he'd left on my flesh. His sharp hiss sounded as he took in the angry blue bruises that covered my cheeks. "You bruise easily, woman."

"A brute manhandled me last night. It makes sense why I would carry bruises of proof come morning. Would you like to see how red and sore you left my cunt, monster?" I asked, not bothering to turn around. His hand landed in my hair, testing my braids. "Maybe you'd like to hurt me more? Come on, puppy, do your fucking worst," I challenged as my eyes closed, and I inhaled his scent.

He dropped my braid and bent down behind me, lifting the sheer material of the dress. I held my breath as his fanned my sore flesh. My hands turned into fists at my sides as I waited for the pain to come, but instead of pain, his lips skimmed over the sore globes of my cheeks. I gasped and spun around, backing up from him while he examined me through heated eyes.

"Don't do that!" I ordered.

"Don't kiss your ass?" he asked gently, letting his gaze drift to the red curls of my sex.

"Exactly," I said as a frown tugged at my lips. I watched him warily as he sat on the bed again, studying me.

"You will come outside and eat with us today. I won't have you hungry while food is available. I don't intend to make you suffer or starve while you are here,

Laura."

"I don't want your food or your hospitality. I want you to free Hope and let her leave here. I can understand you hating me, but she isn't a part of this and has nothing to do with you. Her parents are probably beside themselves searching for her, and Avery will trace her to this place and bring an army down upon you."

"The entire Cheveron bloodline has been neutered of their magic, witch. I made sure of it. I've known where you hid in the mountains for the past forty years, never wandering out of them until just recently. You see, I let my wolf out to track his mate, and I found you teaching adolescent witches to do what exactly? How to work hexes, curse innocent people? How to escape the notice of the humans?" he asked, leaning forward to rest his elbows on his knees as he spoke.

"How did you find me?" I countered, ignoring his question. "I used magic to hide from you, cloaked beneath it to prevent you from discovering the school."

"I let my wolf out to track you and imagine my surprise when I found you deep in the mountains. I told you, you're not the only one with magic. When you thought yourself alone and stared at the stars at night, what was it you wanted most?" he inquired thickly.

"Ooh, this is a bit awkward. I just wanted the ability to masturbate without you," I shrugged, taking a seat in the chair again. "To find a man who could scratch the itch that this curse prevents me from reaching. Any man, really," I continued, noting that his jaw tightened with my response. "Oh, my bad," I winced dramatically. "Did you think I asked the stars for you? Sorry, but no, I just wanted to get off."

"Use me," he offered.

"Hard pass," I retorted. "I don't fuck men who abuse me without my permission. Go fuck someone else, dog."

"How about I bend you over and fuck you like an animal? If my memory is correct, you fucking howl like a bitch in heat when I do you from behind. My thick cock batters those tight walls, the tiny little thing that you are, you took me anyway. Last night I dreamed of you again, but you were this ethereal creature that lured me to your bed, and fuck, did you rock my world. We were in a dark room, and your green eyes glowed with magic when you came with my name on your lips."

"And did the room have a picture above the mantel of a Viking waging war against wolves?" I asked, gazing into his eyes as they narrowed at my question. "That warrior was you in your true form, and those wolves were there to murder me. You protected me from them, even though at the time, you were just like them. That wasn't a dream, Braydon. That was a memory. One you shouldn't have. Pray tell, what did you do to get them? Deals with the devil have consequences."

"I've learned that firsthand, little witch," he laughed coldly.

"I'd like to shower," I said offhandedly.

"There's a natural pool outside, use it," he said through clenched teeth. "I must mark you afterward, though. Unless I fuck you, it will be how I mark you as off-limits to the pack."

"And fucking me would end it, how?" I asked, chewing my lip, studying his mouth as I remembered how it felt in places that craved it. It was too bad he was such an asshole this go-round because he was a master in the bedroom.

"Because my scent would mark your womb as unavailable to the other men here," he said pointedly. "At least until your next breeding cycle," he shrugged.

"Hard pass, again. Show me the pool," I said, standing up.

"No modesty, huh? No complaint about walking out of this room almost naked?" he returned with one brow lifting higher than the other.

"Why would I complain? You enjoy it when I do, and I don't like giving you any enjoyment in this version of you that has returned to me. I can play your villain if you want it to be so, Braydon. You've already assumed the worst of me, so why would I care if your people do the same? I am being debased and made into the monster you accuse me of being, so why fight it?"

"As you wish, follow me," he snapped, standing to open the door.

I followed closely behind him, ignoring the stares of the people who scrutinized me as I emerged from his house. There were several houses around us, each one minimal in structures that had been camouflaged to blend into the scenery. Men, women, and children paused as I passed them. It wasn't until a child spoke that I paused, listening carefully.

"That is the wicked witch?" she asked her mother. I turned, studying the dirty child as her mother pulled her closer to her and made the sign of the cross over her ample bosom. "She doesn't look wicked; she looks pretty."

"She's the witch who cursed our alpha, Haley."

I smirked, knowing that everyone here assumed I was the monster he had told them I was. Let them think what they wanted; I'd stopped caring centuries ago what the world thought of me or my kind. Men stared openly at me when we passed them, and if Braydon saw, he did nothing to sway them to look elsewhere. Once we reached the pond, he took a seat on a large boulder and produced a knife and a piece of wood. My gaze examined him as he started to carve into it.

Pulling off the gown, I stepped into the water, ignoring him as I submerged my body into the chilled water. Judging from the lack of tracks, it was obvious that no one else bathed in the pond. That meant he was forcing me into it to be an asshole. When it felt as if enough time of ignoring him had passed, I turned, staring up at the blue sky as I slowly walked out of the water, aware that leeches had stuck to my flesh. My hand lowered, pulling the few I could reach off as I stopped in front of him, dropping them back into the water.

I didn't move to dress immediately. I stood before him, gazing up at the bright blue sky that often had reminded me of his beautiful eyes, but instead of finding it pretty, it offered nothing but regret. I could feel the weight of his stare on me and dropped my gaze to his, walking past him in silence. Once I dressed, he walked me back to the room. There, he pulled a leech off my back and tossed it into a bucket. Too late, I realized my error, and the reasoning for having me bathe in the water hit me.

"You did that to get my blood?" I asked carefully.

"It's needed for the spell we will use to rid me of you," he admitted with a slight shrug. "I probably will need a lot more than this."

"Why not just take it, mutt?" I questioned harshly. "Give me a knife, and I'll freely give it to you," I suggested, and when he held one out and stepped away from me, I held his stare, using the blade to slit my wrist to the bone, staring at it in horror as it didn't heal immediately.

"Jesus, woman," he snapped, moving to take the knife from me as I held my arm over the bucket, letting the blood pool into it.

"Believe it or not, I want out of this too." My blood pooled into the bucket steadily as I watched it. "If blood is what you want or need to give your witch, take it all."

"And you say I am the one who goes mad?" he snarled as he grabbed my wrist and held it closed. He ripped his shirt off, holding it to the wound as the world spun around me. "Laura?" he whispered as my head rolled back. "Fuck!" he growled, catching me before I hit the floor and everything went black.

CHAPTER SEVEN

Voices speaking in a hushed tone woke me from my sleep. Braydon and Moira spoke at the foot of the bed, their tone reminiscent of lovers. A vile taste coated my mouth, and I held the urge to vomit in.

"You're wrong if you think she isn't evil," he argued.

"She doesn't appear to be evil, nor does she embrace this curse that is also affecting her. You said she cannot take pleasure from another, who would ever place a curse upon themselves to endure centuries of celibacy? She is beautiful and a woman with needs. I can smell it on her. Her arousal is heady and seductive. I get aroused around her, Braydon. Hell, I want to mount her, and I don't even have a cock. You marked her because of it. The younger one, she smells nothing like this one. Laura smells of a woman in full ovulation who hasn't bred in centuries. That means she hasn't been with a man in all that time. She isn't fighting you, and if she was evil as you say she is, wouldn't she fight to escape? Hope says she is sweet, guarded yes, but she has spent centuries training children to live, and that doesn't scream evil witch to me. You assume she is evil, but she's also cursed, alpha. You loathe her because every time you fuck another woman, you wish it was she taking your cock. That is her only crime against you. You are her mate, though, which is clear to everyone *but* you. I can smell it, you know. The mark you both carry."

"I don't want her," he countered.

"I know you do, but I don't think she likes you much either. She slit her wrist to give you blood and could have very well perished because of it. If our witches are correct, she can only die by your hand, but yet she passed out from losing too much blood. My guess is that she can die by her hand, and yet everything within her prevents that from happening, or it did until now. I don't know if she even realized she could."

"You have no idea what she is or has done to me. No, we will be mated once this is finished. Our packs are together as they should be. I will keep my word to your father and ensure you are protected."

"I want love, Braydon," she breathed, and the sound of his mouth against hers forced my heart to clench. "I want a man who will look at me as you did to her as she bathed today. You don't see it, but you gaze at her as if she is the moon to your wolf. I need more than just protection from my mate, and I deserve it."

"I am cursed to feel what I do for her," he argued. "I don't want her, do you hear me? I have dreamed of that bitch since I was a mere child. She has haunted my dreams, consumed the wolf within me until he refused to mate with anyone but her. She is a poison that needs to be bled from my system. I didn't choose her; she made me remember her so that in every life I live, it is she that I crave. I shouldn't feel this need to be with her. It is only her magic working on me that makes it so. If I have to take her head from her pretty shoulders, I will. I am no one's puppet, and I sure as fuck don't plan to mate with a witch who got me into this mess, to begin with. Her blood is the key to unlocking the curse, and when I have the curse undone, she will leave here. You and I have protected your pack from the wolves who hunt them; we continue as we have been. Understand this, sweet wolf, I will always protect you." His voice rose as if he wanted me to hear his words.

"And if they cannot remove the mark on your soul, Braydon? You belong to her even without the curse that pulls you to her. Once upon a time, you chose her. You made her your wife."

"Because she's a witch who can use magic against me, I did. I doubt I ever loved her in any lifetime. She is thin and too tiny, breakable. Her hair is the color of the leaves on the trees in fall, and her eyes gaudy green. Her skin is too pale and covered in freckles, and even now carries bruises from me. She barely even has tits, Moira. I enjoy lusty women who are built to be savaged, and she has nothing to make a man crave her. What man in their right mind would want something so tiny?"

I swallowed past the closing of my throat as I fought the blow to my ego. Many men had wanted me over the centuries, and I'd craved this asshole instead of them. I had kings kneel at my feet. They promised me the world if I lay with them, and I'd wanted this brainless caveman. That made me the biggest idiot in the room.

"If you don't mind, trying to die in peace here," I muttered, pulling the blankets up over my head to hide the tears.

"It's my room, witch," he sneered.

"Then please, send me anywhere else. Fuck, tie me to a fucking tree, and set the bitch on fire if it gets you off. I've had the pleasure of being burned at the stake twice already, and I think I prefer the bite of flames to your company anyway," I chuckled. "And for your information, the King of England loved my tits. He even offered to remove his queen's head if I let him taste them once. The Bastard King of Scotland also begged to taste my flesh, but I refused him, a pity that, since he has the longest tongue of all the kings I served. I wish I could have ridden his face just once and felt it, though I may not have ever gotten off on his mouth."

"You were alive when the Bastard King of Scotland lived?" Moira asked in a shocked tone.

"A downside of being cursed to live forever, I'm afraid," I said harshly from where I hid beneath the covers. "I may be tiny, but I assure you, I am made to endure even the worst brutes that walk this earth, current company included. So is there a tree available? Preferably not one your dog has pissed on since piss makes the fire smell worse as it burns the flesh."

"No one is burning you at the stake, witch," he snapped.

"Damn, can't say I didn't try." I closed my eyes as the door opened and closed, and I exhaled in relief until he ripped the blankets from the bed. I refused to look at him or see the disinterest burning in his gaze from my less than desirable assets. "Can I help you, puppy?" I asked, staring at the wall.

"I told you I would need to replace my scent, and

since the entire male population can smell your pussy dripping with the need to be fucked, I will," he snapped.

"Jack off in a jar and bring it to me, wouldn't want my tiny cunt to disappoint you, now would we?" I laughed silently.

Braydon yanked my feet without warning. He held my legs apart while he began crawling up the bed to settle between them. I watched him through angry eyes as my annoyance rose, and anger pulsed through me. He started working his pants, unbuttoning them. I kicked him in the face without warning, turning to move back up the bed as he howled in anger.

"Fucking hell, Laura, stop!" he snarled, grabbing me again, catching my leg with his hand as the other touched his face. I sat up, punching him with everything I had left in me as he took it, smiling coldly through the blood that pooled from his broken nose. I scrambled backward, but he caught my leg again, tightening his grip on it until I cried out in pain. "You want it rough, little girl, I can be rough," he promised with a voice that wasn't all his.

He threw me onto my stomach, slamming down on top of me, knocking the wind from my lungs as he held me there. His teeth sank into my shoulder, and I screamed out as pain ripped through me. His hand gripped my hair, baring my neck, which he savaged next. A sob exploded from my chest as he nudged my legs apart and began rubbing his cock through the slit of flesh. I spun around, sinking my nails into his shoulder as I tried to cross my legs. Pounding started on the locked door, but he ignored it, backhanding me to stop my assault. Stars erupted in my vision as I lay there, waiting for him to rape me. More pounding started before the door burst open, and men flooded the room along with Moira.

"Jesus, Braydon!" she hissed as she took in the damage to each of us.

"She started it," he warned. "This isn't your fucking business, woman."

"You would rape her?" she asked, and he turned to stare down at me, finding me trembling, bloodied, and naked with him poised to enter my body. "You are the alpha of this pack, and you lead it by example. Do not do this; look at her! Look at her, Braydon. She is bleeding and terrified. Who is the one forcing who now?" she snapped without fear.

"Get out," he warned. "Get out!" he shouted, and she held firm even as the men with her did as he said. "I will not rape her, get out."

My eyes closed in relief or swelling, whichever one it was didn't matter. My body trembled uncontrollably as he watched it. My body ached from his assault, as his no doubt did from mine. I remained unmoving as Moira left the room, closing the broken door in her wake.

"If you attack me, witch, I will retaliate in the same manner," he warned. "I am the alpha, and my wolf considers your fighting foreplay. Do not do it again."

I remained silent as blood threatened to choke off my airway. When he moved back and released me, I turned to spit it from my mouth. My scalp ached from where he'd torn my hair out; he gasped as he took in the damage to my neck and shoulder and swore violently. The pressure of the bed eased as he left it, only for the door to open and close, and then do so again.

Cold hands touched me. I shivered violently as

Moira spoke. "You can't fight him; his wolf won't let him allow it. He is the alpha here, and cannot appear weak." She requested items from someone else in the room and then examined the damage to the back of my neck. "These bites are deep," she continued, even though I didn't respond. "The moss will prevent them from bleeding if you leave it on. Your face, though, that will bruise badly. Is there anything you need, Laura?"

"To escape him and this place," I whispered. "I have to get out of here. Hope has to get out of here before the madness overcomes him. You think this is bad, wait until his berserker comes out to play. It doesn't tire, doesn't feed, and doesn't stop taking what it wants. The last time we triggered the curse was the worst one. Braydon's berserker took me for a fortnight straight, never stopping to see what he'd done to me. It broke me, made me bleed, and I almost died before I finally killed it. If it comes again, no one here will be safe from it. If I am gone, he will follow me when the madness overcomes him. You say you care about your people, then free me to escape their home so that when the curse is triggered, they're spared his wrath."

"No one here will aid you in escaping him," she clucked her tongue. I heard his snort from the other room and closed my eyes. "He is kind and just as alpha of this pack. He doesn't lose his temper, not until you came here."

"I didn't come here. He brought me here. I don't want him, and I sure as hell don't want to be here. I am the Queen of the Witches of the North, Moira. I rule a coven of both dark and light magic witches, combined with the strength of the King of the Vampires of the

Inland Northwest. Do you honestly think they will sit around and do nothing while his only child and I are missing?"

"No, but I also don't think you understand where you are, either. We use magic to protect this village by placing confusion spells to prevent it from being found. Now turn over and stop threatening me so I can prevent your flesh from scarring too horribly."

"You think anything you do can scar my flesh?" I laughed emotionlessly. "I have been burned at the stake twice until my flesh melted from my bones, drowned nine times by priests for my supposed wickedness, and then stoned to death at their hands because I found their efforts cute. I have counseled kings and queens alike who betrayed me and watched kingdoms rise and fall to the whim of churches who took my head three times beside the queens I counseled. I have been beaten, abused, and cursed by my mother for betraying my coven and my order to assassinate that monster in the other room. I ripped her fucking heart out and cursed her to drown in the River Styx for eternity. Do you think I care about myself? I assure you, I do not. I will, however, raze your entire fucking pack to the ground if they harm one hair on that child's head. In all my time alive, I have never broken a vow. I vowed to protect Avery's daughter at all costs, and I made that vow to the only woman I have ever liked. So you with your faked kindness can get the fuck away from me." I sat up, uncaring that blood ran down my body from Braydon's bites.

He entered the room, observing me.

"There is nothing that can kill me but him. Trust me, I've tried it a time or two," I whispered harshly. "You must get creative if you plan to murder me, woman."

"But I can, and I bit you, Laura. You're bleeding out, and if you're dead, I have no use for Avery's daughter, now do I?" he uttered, watching as realization slammed into me.

I laughed until it sounded almost hysterical. He'd fucking done it. He'd savaged me until my life hung in the balance. He watched me as Moira backed up.

"Well, look at you, finally growing a nut sack. Good for you, puppy," I snorted before more laughter took hold of me while blood soaked the bed. "Finally," I wheezed while tears slipped from my eyes to slowly race down my cheeks. He watched me through narrowed eyes while I held his heavy stare. "About time you finished this."

"She's positively mad," she whispered in a horrified tone.

"Ready the moss," he snapped, moving toward me. "If you fight me, you will die. If you die, I will snap that girl's neck and leave her corpse to feed the wildlife so that her parents never get closure and never know what happened to either of you. Do you understand me, Laura? Avery will never find either of you and will spend the rest of her life searching for you."

"Or you can free her, and let me die and end this," I breathed. "Let me go, and just end this for us both. All you have to do is walk out that door and let this happen."

"And allow you to make me into the monster you are? No, thank you. You will survive this, and I will find another way to end the curse that doesn't include ending your life," he said, slowly moving toward me. I flinched when he got too close, recoiling as if his presence alone was an assault. "I won't hurt you."

"No?" I laughed as my nose bled, dripping down my naked chest. "You always hurt me. It is part of the curse. Eventually, you will destroy me. You won't be a monster if you end my life, not really. Let me die, Braydon. Just let me go so I can know peace."

"Not happening," he hissed, sitting behind me, carefully pulling my naked form against his. "Use the moss, Moira. Secure it to her bites, and then bring the salve for her face and legs," he ordered.

His hand turned my head, baring my neck for her to secure the moss to the bite. They forced tonics down my throat as more and more people entered the room until consciousness escaped me, and darkness took hold.

"You will not die here, I promise you that, littlest witch," he uttered as I gave in to the darkness that beckoned me to it.

CHAPTER EIGHT

An entire week passed without seeing Braydon since the fight. He didn't come to check on me, and I didn't ask for him. Moira came and went in silence, never speaking to me after I'd threatened the life of her pack. I didn't eat the food she brought and didn't drink the tonic which she placed by the bed every night, to escape the nightmares that haunted me.

I was rudely informed about just how much I stunk by the healer. She'd forced me to bathe and applied lavender to the bath to make me stink less like rotting flesh, according to her. Her beady brown eyes studied me, and yet the bites hadn't healed on my shoulder or my neck. Either no one had realized that they were the bite of an alpha claiming his mate before now, or they were choosing to keep that knowledge to themselves. However, the ancient crone of a healer hissed as she revealed the wound, clucking her tongue at the damage.

"So, this is why you summoned me? To look at the alpha's claiming mark? She is claimed and dying because he left her."

"It's not a mating mark, he just bit her because they were fighting," Moira countered. "It isn't! That is not allowed to happen. It's barbaric and can end in the death of the female wolf. My father abolished that practice when he only sired daughters. Braydon wouldn't mark her; he intends to be my mate, eventually."

"He didn't mark her, child. His wolf claimed her as its mate. Braydon wouldn't have control over it any more than she would. The wolf can sense what the human doesn't, and I assure you, this is its mark. That is why it isn't healing. He may have claimed her, but he didn't finish biblically claiming her, which means she is not long for this earth. If he doesn't finish it, she will die. That mark is a poison if he abandons her without finishing the mating ritual."

"You're saying she has to fuck him?" she snarled.

"Or you can watch her die. I suggest you notify him of the mark he placed on her and see how he wants to proceed."

"He doesn't want her dead," Moira argued, more to herself than to the healer.

I exhaled slowly, closing my eyes. "Make sure Hope gets freed because the moment magic is restored, no confusion backwater magic spell will protect you from Conner Halverson and Avery Cheveron. You will run for the rest of your lives as they hunt you down one by one until not one wolf remains of your pack. That's not a threat; it's a fact. Now get out," I hissed weakly as I rested my head against the pillow to sleep.

"She doesn't have long," the healer said, ignoring me.

"Braydon released his wolf to run off steam."

"I suggest you tell the boys to go fetch the alpha. She will be dead before the sun rises in the morning without him. Her immortality has prolonged the inevitable, but she isn't healing, nor will she unless he finishes claiming her. His venom has been slowly killing her, and it's reached the end of its cycle."

"I'll send them, but if she dies, it won't be the worst thing, would it?" she whispered.

"You think she lies? Even now, creatures are scouring the bayou for her and that girl. She's hexed to be neutered magically, but eventually, that will end. Every hex has an out, just as every curse has a cure. Once she triggers it, she will be powerful. I've heard of her before, as have the other witches in the bayou. She isn't some weak witch to be messed with, Moira. She's a Cheveron witch, born of the blood of Hecate herself. You might as well have walked in and slapped Lucifer in the face and tried to get away with it without consequences. Right now, her friend, as she calls her, who is also a Cheveron witch, is out there searching for the other fucking Cheveron witch we hold. He brought in some of the most powerful witches, and while we hold the cards now, we won't for long. Pray she does not die, for if she does, I doubt Avery would go away quietly into the night. If he hadn't bitten her, I'd free her and that girl myself to protect this pack."

"I'll tell the boys to find him immediately. Keep her alive until he returns. We can worry about the others later."

It was hours before I awoke again after listening to the healer inform Moira of just how screwed they were when something caught my attention. My eyes opened as a groan slipped past my lips. Death by wolf-bite sucked ass. Blue eyes glowed from the shadows of the room, and I paused, staring into them as a wolf slowly stepped into the candlelight. It was huge, immensely larger than the one that had guarded the door, or walked us to this place upon being captured.

I moaned as I moved back, trying to put distance between us as it slowly crept forward with its head lowered as if it hunted me.

"Good doggy, don't eat me, please," I whispered the barely audible words, unable to make myself speak louder. Whatever they'd put in the tonics they'd forced me to drink had me seeing double and worse, I was pretty sure I was drugged. The wolf looked familiar, and yet I couldn't place him while high on their tonics. Not that it really mattered since I was dying, and the thought of it terrified me. Facing mortality wasn't something I'd ever had to worry about, not until now. Thinking or saying death could happen was one thing; knowing it was coming, well, it was terrifying. "Oh, this is really going to suck," I croaked as I felt the bed at my back, and the moss dropped from my shoulder, exposing the raw flesh that had spider-webbed where the poison had spread.

The wolf jumped onto the bed, and I yelped as my hands bunched into the blankets and I closed my eyes, praying to whatever God would hear me as it bared its teeth and sniffed the mark.

"Our Father, who art in heaven, hallowed be thy name. Thy kingdom come; they will be done…" I paused as the wolf licked my shoulder, pulling me from the prayer to the current situation. I didn't care which

God heard or protected me and was covering all my bases. "I'm not good to eat, I promise. I'm boney and too thin. I probably taste like the wicked witch, and I don't care what anyone says, witches do *not* taste like chicken. Please don't eat me, be a good wolf, and go find someone else to eat, please?" I whispered. "On earth as it is in heaven. Lead me not into temptations yadda, yadda, yadda, or however this thing goes, and I'll bake you some bread…" My head tilted with the wrongness of the words. I hadn't said a prayer since the early 1300s, and it was showing because I was pretty sure Jesus didn't want me to bake him anything. "I invoke thee and call upon you, Hecate. Mother of us all, hear my prayer, and hear my call. Take my soul from this wretchedness; feed my magic back into the well of my bloodline and protect them through the hardest times; of this, I request of thee. I call upon thee to bring me home. Hear my prayer, hear my call, take me past the pain and wrath, and take me where my soul can rest, I invoke thee. Okay, doggie, let's do this."

I opened my eyes, staring into ice-blue glaciers that studied me. The wolf licked my shoulder again, and I nodded to it. My vision blurred as everything seemed to spin around me, which indicated I was seconds away from passing out and being spared feeling the painful bite of his strong jaws.

"Go ahead, but for the record, going out as puppy chow is an all-time low way to die, even for me, puppy," I uttered as I prepared to cross the veil and face whatever awaited me there. I wouldn't give this beast the satisfaction of me closing my eyes as it devoured me, either. I'd face it and its razor-sharp teeth head-on with what little strength I had left. "Are you sure you're not a hellhound that Hades sent up to help me? He owes me a favor. I gave him an eternal source of power when I cursed my mother to drown in his river." The wolf stared at me, and I could have sworn it was smiling at my words. "Well, get on with it. It's impolite to keep a woman waiting, beast."

Magic rippled through the room, and I gasped as Braydon appeared where the wolf sat. It kind of deflated the irony of being puppy chow when a naked Viking with perfectly blunt teeth hovered over me.

"Hellhound?" he asked, as his eyes lowered to the nasty wound on my shoulder.

"It seemed perfectly reasonable considering you were licking me?" I said, somehow forming the answer as a question. "*You!*" I hissed weakly. "You fucking bit me. You pussy, you missed my artery."

"So I did, little witch," he agreed. "Now, it seems I have to give you the serum to save you."

"I'm okay with dying," I lied. "I've said my prayers and everything. I'm ready."

"You said them wrong," he countered as he settled between my thighs, pushing them apart. "You're really horrible at praying."

"I'm a pagan," I shrugged and then winced as pain shot through me. "You know that when you're not near me, I don't feel pain, right?"

"You're dying," he announced.

"I know," I returned weakly. "By your hand or teeth, per se. Fitting, wouldn't you agree?"

"I have no intention of letting you die, little witch."

"Stop calling me that. My name is Laura."

"I will need you to be a good girl for me and don't fight me on this. I will tie you to the bed and do whatever it takes to save you."

"I don't want your *serum*," I spat out hoarsely.

"Yes, you do, because right now everything inside of you is screaming to survive. Everything you are and everything that created you demands you fight to live. You're a born witch, from the first line of witches, Laura. You may not be afraid of death, but you want the cure so you can live, and I have it right here. Tell me I'm wrong. Tell me to walk out that door and let you die."

I opened my mouth to speak, to say the words that would send him away, but I couldn't. I didn't want to die. I had to live, and he was right, everything inside of me screamed to let him help me. The problem was, it meant allowing him to have me, and by doing so, I'd be mated to his wolf.

"Drink," he said, holding up a vial of blue liquid. When I just stared at it, he continued. "You're about to be fucked five ways from Sunday, and you're rather tiny and weak, witch. You want to survive it, drink the fucking potion."

"What's in it? And I'm not that tiny, ya know? You have fucked me far worse than you could ever imagine. You remember nothing in berserker form, and I assure you, it's much rougher than your wolf can ever hope to accomplish. You've bruised my womb before, jerk."

He smirked. "I'll bruise it again, promise," he said huskily. "Drink the fucking poison; it's a pain reliever and concoction that will help you through the bonding of souls."

"I don't particularly even like you, let alone your

soul right now." His eyes smiled as he watched me tip up the vile and sniff the liquid. "It smells like ass."

"It probably tastes like it too, bottoms up," he growled, sitting back as he watched me. "You're in heat, woman," he grumbled, scrubbing his hand down his face.

"I've been in heat since the moment my mother activated the curse, jerk. I am perpetually held in my greatest time of need without the ability to get off. It was my mother's greatest achievement to leave me in a state of need that could never be fulfilled until you came back. It is how you find me, by the scent of my need." I tipped the vail up, drinking it. He reached out for it, and our fingers touched, sending sparks shooting up my arm.

"How did you meet me, Laura?" he asked, his eyes guarded as if he wasn't sure he wanted to know the story. As if once he heard it, he could not forget it.

"My mother sent me out to eradicate a ship of Vikings that had come ashore in England and met with foul play. You had been mortal and yet bitten by werewolves and left to die. I was dispatched to end you. When I reached you, you were tending to the children who had been attacked. I could have whispered a spell and ended you easily, but something about you stopped me. You cared for the weak, this immense Viking warrior who was covered in battle scars, tending to these dying little whelps. It was unheard of back then, especially for the monsters of the North. You knew I watched you, and yet you didn't fear me. You challenged me every night, standing at the shore, protecting the children from the monster who watched you from the shadows. One night

I slipped from the woods and made my way to where you stood, and you smiled at me. I was one of the most powerful witches of my time, and here was this brave Viking who just smiled at me as if he knew a secret I wasn't privy to. Monsters had cowered in my presence, praying to their gods for mercy, but not you. You smiled, and when I asked you to close your pretty blue eyes so I could end your life, you told me no. You told me that if I was going to kill you, I had to have the balls to look into your eyes as I took your life," I recalled, telling it to him through what I remembered.

"But you didn't kill me," he pointed out.

"No, you kissed me," I whispered as the memories replayed in my mind. I laughed as silent tears slipped from my eyes. "You kissed me and told me I was the most beautiful thing you had ever seen before. I slapped you, for I'd never been kissed before, and yet I kissed you back. To you, it was hilarious, but for me, it was confusing. I'd felt nothing like it, and as a pure-born witch, I wasn't allowed to consort with men. So I left you on the beach to watch you from the woods once more. I was there naked for a blessing to gain the strength to do what I was sent to do when you came into the forest. Your boldness startled me, but then I peered into your Nordic eyes, and everything changed. I drowned within their endless depths, and instead of freezing in their icy fjords, I felt warmth. You pushed me up against a tree and promised to be gentle with me, which you weren't. We were happy together and married in secrecy."

Braydon watched me through wary eyes. "You don't need all the details of how we fell in love, I guess. You fucked me and told me I was yours forever. I went home to tell my mother that I had finished the job after hiding you and your people from mine. They accosted me the moment the lie left my lips. I was beaten, tortured, and then my mother told me they had found you. They brought you into the room, bloodied and broken. They sealed us in, and I was told what would happen by my mother. That because I was a whore for you, I would know little else from you other than lust and pain. You were born a berserker then bitten by a wolf. They used a spell to make it the same, fueled by blind madness once the trigger is pulled by our bond as soulmates. Once the madness takes you, you become purely berserker and nothing else. Your target was always me, to take me until my death, or until I killed you. It mattered little to them, which came first as long as we suffered. So my mother watched you fuck me, brutally.

"You weren't you, but to me, it was as if they'd changed my gentle warrior into my worst nightmare. You left no part of me untouched. For weeks you attacked me, sleeping wasn't something you did. I begged you, pleading with you to stop. I hurt so fucking bad that my body refused to work. I was nothing to you, not human, not the woman you claimed to love. I was an enemy, a battle your berserker had to win. So when I struggled against you and put my arms up to hold you off, you broke them. When I used my legs to keep you at a distance, you broke them too. When I lay there defenseless, taking what you did to me, knowing it would never stop, I whispered a spell to end your life, so igniting the curse upon us both. Weeks, weeks of me being brutalized, having whispered every spell I knew to undo the curse, knowing that the moment I took your life, I'd wish for death myself, I did what they had known I would. I killed the one man I have ever given my heart to. I had healed from you breaking my limbs, which my mother hadn't noticed as she'd watched you night after night, fucking me. So when she came into the cage where we were held, I ripped her fucking heart out because that is what it had felt like when I had killed you. I cursed her soul to Hades, to drown in the River Styx for all eternity. That way, she knew what I felt like without you. So, Braydon, I can withstand being savaged by you because it is all I have ever known."

"That's not a pretty story," he uttered, rubbing his fingers over my thigh.

"No, but it's ours."

CHAPTER NINE

Braydon paced at the foot of the bed like a caged beast waiting to be set free. His body was a wealth of sinewy muscles that clenched with every move he made. My eyes feasted on him, lost in the graceful, raw beauty of his body. My hands absently lowered to my thighs as I sat on the bed, staring at him with my hair free of the braids the healer had undone as she'd bathed me. My shoulder ached, burning for him, and he paused as if he felt my discomfort.

"What are you waiting for?" I asked absently, more to myself than to him. He was like a starving beast, and yet he waited for something to happen. The concoction he'd had me drink renewed my strength and my mind. No longer hazy or on death's door because of the potion I'd swallowed, I watched him pacing.

A foreboding filled me as those sinfully blue eyes turned, trailing over my body with a liquid fire that threatened to consume me. A shiver of unease slid through me as heat pooled to my apex. Swallowing hard, I opened my mouth to speak, but only a soft moan escaped past my dry lips.

"What exactly was in that potion?" I questioned as heat rolled through my body, and my nipples pebbled to hard peaks. His gaze lowered to them, slowly drifting down to my naked flesh.

"Something to lessen the pain of our mating, witch. It also gave you the strength to participate," he growled huskily. "I'm about to fuck you, hard. I've dreamed of this moment since the first time my dick got hard as a youth. Every pussy I've savaged was yours, every mouth I've tasted paled in comparison to yours. Do you have any idea how fucked up that is? I would eat a pussy and find it bland, wanting what yours promised to be. I'd fuck a maiden only to call out your name instead of hers in the throes of passion. Your pretty eyes haunt my every dream, and I'm about to fuck you out of my system. I may mate you because the wolf within me demands it, but that doesn't mean you will be mine, understand?"

"You say the sweetest shit, puppy," I groaned as heat fanned my flesh. "Climb on, then, let's get it over with, shall we?" I asked, slowly slipping my fingers to my sex, watching his icy stare following it with a predator's glint.

I was already wet, swollen with the need to come. My back arched into my touch, even though I felt nothing and wouldn't unless he was touching me. My other hand lifted, cradling my small breasts, which he said he found lacking, and yet his tongue traced his full bottom lip with hunger.

"Come on, wolf boy, show me what you got," I taunted, watching his intense stare as it lifted, locking with mine in a silent battle.

"Soon," he grumbled, scrubbing his hand down his face.

I leaned back, letting my legs drop open to his steely gaze. He smirked, watching me carefully as my hands trembled with the concoction running through me. I was bolder than I'd been in the past, never having taunted this warrior to bed, and yet I wanted him to ravish me. I needed it as I needed the air that filled my lungs. A fire was kindling within me, and I had a feeling that his potion had more than just a pain reliever in it.

"Do you know how wolves mate, Laura?" he asked softly as he moved toward the bed, grabbing my ankles to brush his thumbs over them.

"You've never asked me that before or told me. You've never even shown me your wolf. I'm not a wolf, in the case that it has slipped your mind," I replied carefully. I gasped as he yanked me to the edge of the bed, kneeling between my legs.

"Good, I prefer the element of surprise," he chuckled wickedly, letting his tongue dance over the inside of one thigh before doing it to the other. A shiver of lust rushed through me while his eyes held mine. His sinful tongue lavished my flesh without touching the one place I needed it the most. "Give me your hands, woman," he growled.

"No," I whispered breathlessly. My nipples were painfully erect, and my sex dripped with arousal for him.

"No?" he returned as a lethal smile crossed his mouth.

"I didn't stutter, did I?" I hissed.

One minute he was before me, and the next I was flat on my stomach with my hands held behind my back. I could feel the leather of his belt he'd grabbed from his dresser as he used it to bind them together. Once he'd finished, he didn't let me up. His hand cradled the globe of my ass, slowly working the flesh with his hand. When he lifted it away from me, I exhaled only to cry out as his hand slapped against my ass cheek. He rubbed it gently after the assault, which turned the pain to pleasure. I held my breath, knowing more was to come. I wasn't wrong. His hand landed harder, and I moaned the moment he began to massage my stinging flesh. Fingers pushed against my opening, and I squirmed against the bed. His husky laugh sent a fresh wave of need shooting to my molten center.

"Bad girls get spanked, Laura. Are you a good girl or a bad girl?" His tone was dark, filled with gravel that made it sound like sex dripping from his lips. His finger pushed into my body, and I whimpered, pushing back against it to take more. "You're fucking soaked, little witch," he growled. "If I didn't know any better, I'd say you enjoy being spanked."

He slapped my ass again, watching me squirm against his hold, which only sent his finger deeper into my core. Another pushed into my body, and I teetered on the edge of a storm. My body tightened, clenching against the fingers that fucked me slowly, unhurriedly. My legs spread apart; turning my head, I stared up at him where he watched the pink spreading across my ass cheek. I lifted to my knees, giving him full access to my most private parts.

Wintery eyes locked with mine in a silent battle

before a slow smile spread over his sinful lips. He pushed the dark blonde hair away from his face and sat back on his haunches, staring at me as if I was a gift he didn't know how to accept.

"You're tiny," he said irritably.

I glared at him, hating that he thought me delicate. So what if I was barely over five feet tall, or weighed less than the women I'd seen around here? My curves weren't generous, and I'd come to terms with my rather lacking attributes, but then I'd had several lifetimes to do so.

"You know, you could just finish yourself off as you did before, pushing your come into my body without ever having to fuck my less than average pussy. I wouldn't want you to have to strain yourself by fucking me when you find me and my tiny tits so unappealing. Untie me, now," I whispered through trembling lips. "Untie me!" I screamed as I rolled away from him and sat on the edge of the bed, breathing through the anger that burned through me. "Just do it without me, and we will figure it out."

"No, it doesn't work like that, Laura."

"Make it!" I hissed venomously. "You don't want me, that much is apparently clear. So do whatever it is you need to do and get the fuck out. Go back to running in the woods or whatever it is you were doing."

"I have to mate with you, or the bite on your shoulder and neck will kill you," he snapped.

"And?" I laughed emotionlessly.

"And I won't have your blood on my hands."

"Another wolf can do this. I've heard it doesn't have to be the one who bit the female. Bring in someone else," I whispered thickly. "Anyone else," I suggested coldly. So his insult to my self-esteem had cut a little deeper than I'd thought, but this was my Braydon. The man I'd endured the curse to be with, even if only for the short time before it played out, and this time, he found me utterly pathetic and lacking.

His hand touched my shoulder, and I jerked away, standing up to face him. He watched my chest rise and fall with my labored breathing. He stood up slowly, stalking me until my back slammed against the wall, and I turned, only for him to push me against it.

"If you think I'm calling in anyone else to fuck your tight cunt, you're wrong, witch. You are mine; do you hear me? Not mine until I decide otherwise or to throw you away, mine to protect and care for. I do fucking hate your tiny tits. I hate the way they get hard the moment I look at them. I hate the way they feel in my mouth and against my tongue, and I really fucking hate the fact that I crave them to be there. I hate that you're fucking tiny when all I want to do is savagely bend you over and fuck you until my knot is buried so deeply within you I can't get it out, and I don't think I'd fucking even want to. I hate the way your scent drives my wolf wild and makes me crave to taste you. You're perpetually in fucking heat, which means from the moment I captured you, I've wanted nothing else but to fuck you. Lacking, no. Tiny, yes," he snapped harshly. "I want to push you down and force my cock into that dirty mouth of yours, but it won't fit. I want to use you in the worst fucking way, and I know that if I do, I will hurt you."

His hand threaded through my hair as his mouth skimmed against the back of my neck, slowly kissing it as his legs spread mine apart. His engorged erection touched against my spine, and I moaned at the silken length that I craved more than air.

"You won't break me, Viking. Hurt me, yes. You forget I like it rough," I groaned as he kissed the base of my spine, slowly working his way down until his breath fanned my arousal-soaked core.

He chuckled before his tongue dragged through the wetness, and a groan escaped his lips. "You taste like sin, woman." His mouth ravished my core hungrily, like he couldn't get enough. I cried out as he used my hair to turn me around in a swift move that had me pinned against the wall so his mouth could suckle one breast and then the other. His fingers once against found my apex and slowly rubbed the sensitive flesh until I was gyrating against him as my body sang with need. "Fucking hell, woman," he groaned as he found my mouth, claiming it with fervor while his tongue demanded entrance. I moaned from the pleasure of his fingers that skimmed over my swollen flesh as he dominated the kiss.

Pulling away from me, he stared into my eyes. "You're wicked, woman," he uttered hoarsely as he brought his fingers up and ran them over my lips. "Let this happen; don't fight it," he growled. "Let me have you," he demanded as he picked me up by my hips and walked us backward toward the bed. He dropped me to it, and I whimpered at the motion, unable to catch myself from falling, which caused him amusement as he lay back, staring up at me. "You're absolutely fucking beautiful, little witch."

"Flattery will get you nowhere, wolf," I answered huskily.

He smiled roguishly as he lifted me, adjusting his cock until my wet flesh straddled it. Instinct fueled me, while eyes the color of the clearest seas in winter gazed up at me, I rubbed against him.

"You want that, don't you?" he asked, his hands controlling my hips as my arms remained trapped by his belt behind me. "You want it buried within you until it stretches that tight cunt full. Ask me to fuck you, witch. Tell me to destroy you."

"No," I whispered, watching his mouth curve into a sinful smirk. "I don't beg for anything, Braydon."

"You'll beg me to come," he chuckled huskily. He moved my body faster, watching me as my chest rose and fell while the storm within me grew wild and barreled toward the edge of the cliff, and yet the moment I would have gone over it, he picked me up, stopping me from reaching it. "Mmm, you want that, don't you? To feel that release that only I can bring you to, don't you?"

"Yes," I answered, staring down at his thick cock. "Braydon?" I whispered through dry lips. "Something is way wrong with your penis," I noted.

"It's a knot, little witch. It's about to be buried inside of your tight cunt," he chuckled.

It wasn't normal. He had an overly large cock, to begin with, but the head was purple and enlarged past what I could take. I shook my head while he watched me. Fear trickled up my spine as the denial of what he planned entered my mind. He lifted me carefully, poising it against my entrance soaked with need. I felt it lessening, as if he controlled how thick it was. When I peered back down, it wasn't as large as it had been.

"Look at me, Laura," he demanded.

I did, pulling my wide eyes away from what he had poised to enter my body. He smirked, enjoying the fear that danced from me. He rubbed it against my opening, and I shook my head, fully intending to tell him where he could stick it, but he slammed me down, and I howled as he entered me. My body screamed, burning with the pain of fullness as he held me seated to the base of his cock with no way to escape it. Tears slipped from my eyes as he watched me jerking my hips to withdraw his cock. Muscles that hadn't been used in almost fifty years screamed in agony while he remained still, holding me onto him as his cock grew even larger, filling me.

"Breathe for me, sweet girl," he uttered hoarsely. "You're okay. Relax and just let it happen. It's not even close to being finished growing yet, but you can handle it." He lifted me, staring at where we were joined. His eyes turned to liquid pools of blue flames as he pushed me back down. "You need to come for me."

"Are you serious? You're trying to knot my very human vagina! I'm not a wolf, Braydon. I'm created with human anatomy."

"You're not human, woman. If you were, you'd have died a long time ago. Now be a good girl and ride my cock. I want to watch those pretty green eyes burn with pleasure as you come for me. Come on, stop being a pussy and use yours to take what you want from me," he growled, lifting me only to slam me down harder onto his massive erection.

"It hurts, asshole!" I snapped irritably.

"It's supposed to," he smirked roguishly. His fingers left my hips to pinch my nipples, pulling them roughly as I cried out. "I told you, you're fucking tiny. Do you have any idea how you look sitting atop me, riding my cock with your tight cunt grasping it? You're fucking hot, so fucking hot being my good girl and taking the whole thing. Do you know how many women have taken even the start of my knotted cock? None: none have ever been able to accept it, and yet you, my littlest witch, slid right onto it like a fucking champion. They weren't made for me, but you are. Now fucking take it or I will bend you over and give you more than you can take," he warned, gripping my hips as he helped me place my feet flat upon the bed.

I lifted, dropping my head to watch as his cock spread my flesh painfully. I continued lifting until I cradled it within the base of my flesh, and my eyes rose to his before I slammed down, screaming as pain mixed with pleasure.

"Good girl," he crooned, rocking my hips before lifting my body again to repeat the motion.

Braydon continued, lifting and rocking my body until I was moaning as it hummed with pleasure. Everything inside of me seemed to build in turbulence that I couldn't contain. I was spiraling out of control as he precisely danced me to the edge. My eyes locked with his, sensing he was fully aware of the coming cataclysm that was about to erupt.

He smiled wickedly and growled, his voice escaping his lips in an inhuman, otherworldly tone. "Fuck me, Laura. Come for me, my sweet witch."

I screamed as everything combusted. My body sang as a kaleidoscope of colors filled my vision. It was violent, brutally so as my body trembled while his name escaped my lips over and over. His hands rocked me, using my body to hold me in the orgasm until he couldn't handle it anymore. He picked me up roughly, flipping me onto my belly as he nudged my legs apart from behind. His hand gripped my hair, threading his fingers through it as he yanked it back while pounding into me harder than before with his cock. The pain was delicious through the waves of orgasm I rode blindly.

I bucked against him, sensitive from the orgasm still pushing through me. He didn't stop; his hips slammed against mine without mercy, and I whimpered. His mouth crushed against mine hungrily, nipping my bottom lip that trembled from too many sensations all at once. He snarled gutturally, turning my neck to lick the wound that had yet to heal, and I yelped as he nipped at it, growing painfully large within me as his teeth sank into my shoulder. His cock battered against my womb agonizingly, his teeth held onto my shoulder, and he savagely took me until I felt him tensing against my ass. I growled loudly as his knot grew until I thought it would tear me apart, but he was relentless, holding me down, knotting me without mercy. I whimpered, coming around his cock while it enlarged to seal the entrance of my womb.

Braydon held me still, lapping against the wound he'd reopened. His hand released my hair while his mouth unclasped from my flesh. I fell over moaning as he chuckled behind me, stuck in my body while it clenched around him greedily, taking every ounce of come his cock released. His hands spread my ass cheeks, and I felt him thickening even more. He pulled against me, and I screamed as burning pain ripped through me.

"No," I whimpered as the realization of what he

intended to do hit me. "You'll break me. You will rip me apart, Braydon," I warned through horrified eyes.

"If I don't withdraw from your cunt, I will breed you. He won't stop until you're pregnant. Release my cock from your greedy womb, woman," he snapped through clenched teeth. He peered down at me, as if he'd known all along he'd have to do this. "I may not want you dead, Laura, but I sure as fuck am not putting my child into your womb yet."

"Then do it," I whispered, spreading myself wide as he started to withdraw from my body. My head burrowed into the bed, and a blood-curdling scream escaped. I sobbed while he pulled against the bone within me that held him there, cradled against my womb. Tears burned my eyes as he worked to free his cock from where he'd knotted within me. He jerked, groaning as pain to free his cock hit both of us.

"Your cunt is like a fucking piranha," he groaned.

I lay there, bound and unable to move while he yanked and pulled to free himself, and then pain turned to pleasure, changing into something else entirely as he once again began slamming into me. My eyes dried of the tears as everything within me fought against what he was trying to do. He didn't want a child with me, but I couldn't have children. I was barren, unable to create life because mine wasn't natural.

He came again and yanked roughly, forcing his cock out through the lubrication of his own orgasm. I sobbed as the agony burned, filling my body with an endless throb that wouldn't stop. Trembling started, and my teeth chattered as if the temperature had dropped to freezing inside the room. It was wrong, all of it. Wetness released from my body while pain ripped me apart from within. His hands worked the belt that held my arms, and the moment he freed me, I turned, slapping him hard against his cheek.

"I can't have children, you fucking bastard," I cried before my body released more fluid. I peered down at the blood that covered the bed and whimpered. Rolling into a ball, I sobbed. I would die here, I realized. His blind hatred of me, his unwillingness to stay within me had broken something that couldn't be undone. "I hate you, mutt. I hate you more than I have ever hated anyone!"

Silence filled the room after my sudden outburst. I heard the rapid beat of his heart as my words settled on him. The door opened and closed, and I lay there in a pool of blood as violent tremors rushed through me. When it reopened, it was Moira who entered with Braydon on her heels.

"What did you do to her now?" she demanded.

"I mated with her, that was what you said had to be done, woman. It has to be this way."

"Braydon, tell me you didn't do what I think you did," she hissed, and the sound of her hand meeting his face over and over filled the room. "You monster! Get out! How could you? She's human; you were supposed to fuck her and knot her so that your wolf could prevent her from dying from the poison of its bite. Why would you take the knot out? It isn't done because it can kill the female wolf, and her body is human still!"

"I can't chance her becoming pregnant, Moira. It's too dangerous for her and the babe."

"No? You should have thought about that before

you fucking gave her your bite. You chose her, *you*, Braydon. Your wolf only bites *your* mate. It was acting on instinct; what the fuck is your excuse? First, you bite her, and then you abandon her to be ravished by the poison alone. I sent them out to get you so you could save her. Not fucking knot her and then rip her apart. Get out!"

"She is *my* mate!" he snapped.

"She won't be if she dies because you fucking murdered her! She won't be anyone's mate, now will she? Get out of this room and fetch the healers. She's bleeding out while you argue with me," she hissed violently as more hits sounded. Something cold was pressed between my legs as the darkness took me under, sparing me from the pain that continually rocked through me.

"Thank you," I whispered as everything went dark.

CHAPTER TEN

I awoke to a hand pushing the hair away from my face. My eyes opened to find Hope with me, her eyes filled with tears as she looked me over. I turned, uncaring of my nudity as I sat up, wincing at the swollenness between my thighs and the cramps that assaulted my midsection.

"Are you okay?" I whispered through cracked lips.

"Are you?" she countered thickly as she hugged me. "They brought me in here last week, Laura. You've been sleeping for seven fucking days! Nothing they did would wake you, nothing. They brought in witches, and they couldn't even sense you here, like you were somewhere else entirely. They said your soul was wrong, that it wasn't even here anymore," she sobbed against my shoulder. "I thought I lost you!"

"I'm fine," I assured her, grabbing the blanket to shield myself, only to find I was covered in an oversized shirt that smelled like the mutt. "Are you well? Are you being fed?" I asked hurriedly.

"Yes, Moira is seeing to me and has made sure the

men stay away. She's rather sweet considering she's my jailor," she shrugged as I sat back, staring at her. "I have no magic."

"I know. Braydon made a deal with Thea. You, your mother, and I have no magic, which means no one is coming to save you yet. We've been hexed, is my guess. I think that was why Thea was at the ball, that and she wanted payback for the death of her child. I don't know how far it extends, only that if I was going to go out as she did, I'd hex every witch who I could."

"Hexes have a loophole though, we just have to find it," she said in a hushed tone.

Footsteps sounded through the front of the house. Her violet eyes swung toward the door as Braydon entered it, dripping sweat from his face and naked chest. His gaze searched mine, his knuckles tightening on the ax he held taking a step toward us.

"Do you intend to cut her up too, dog?" Hope sneered, standing as if she intended to defend me with her bare hands.

"No," he growled hoarsely, staring at me through wintery blue eyes.

"Then get out. I believe Moira said she forbid you from hovering at Laura's bed days ago." She crossed her arms, giving him a glare that would melt the bones off a lesser man.

"She's my mate," he challenged.

"The fuck she is, *mutt*. She's my aunt, and if she wanted you, she'd say so." She turned, looking at me for direction.

"I don't want him," I croaked out, turning to look for water to wet the dryness of my mouth. "Water?" I whispered. He refused to leave, and when he stepped closer, she hissed and opened her mouth to scream while his eyes narrowed on her stubbornness.

"Moira!" Hope shouted toward the open door.

Moira entered with a raised brow, moving her eyes between Hope and Braydon before they settled on me. "You're alive?" she asked, clapping her hands to the wolf that stood guard. "I need the tonic from the fridge, now," she instructed, and when he refused to budge from his position just outside my door, she turned to Braydon with a pointed look.

"Get it now," he growled. He backed up to the wall, dropping the ax against it, watching me. "You slept for an entire fucking week, witch."

"Pity it wasn't forever," I muttered hoarsely.

A pitcher of something was brought in and handed to Moira, who moved to the bedside and poured a small glass full. I reached for it eagerly and ignored her warning to drink slowly. The moment it hit my stomach, I gagged, putting my hand against my mouth while I closed my eyes against the need to retch it up.

"She needs a bath with the herbs I gathered, and since you refuse to allow her out of this hovel you call home, you must bring the basin in here so I can bathe her. Your other choice is to take her outside the barrier unless you wish to force the poor girl to wash in our drinking water again to be an asshole?" she asked.

"Get the old tub into the main room," he told the guard. "Bring me water, I will heat it by the fire for her myself," he snapped, crossing his arms to stare at Moira as if he dared her to challenge his orders. When no one argued, he relaxed.

"I need to check her," Moira stated to the room. No one moved from their spot while she approached the bed. "I'm about to examine her vagina, so those of you who need not be here should wait outside." No one moved. "Both of you, get out, and you too!" she shouted at the guard, shooing them out until we were alone. Her soft eyes turned to look at me with pity.

"Why do you even care?" I asked, uncertain why she out of everyone here cared at all. Braydon was supposed to be her mate, and yet he'd bitten me. It connected our souls on a deeper level than she could ever hope to achieve, and yet she refused to let me die or be abused.

"I don't," she lied.

"You do, because if you didn't, I'd be dead right now."

"Men who abuse women have a special place in hell, Laura. I should know more than most." She pulled down the blankets and indicated with her hands that I should lay back.

I hesitated before doing as she asked. "What happened?" I asked.

"It's personal," she returned.

"You're about to have your face next to my vagina, therefore personal seems to be a moot point." I placed my arms behind my head as she pushed my legs apart.

"I was raped by my mate, bitten, and knotted. He hunted my pack and me slaughtering anyone he smelled on my flesh. My father was mortally wounded in the attack, and he called upon Braydon as alpha of this pack to defend us; the price was my hand in marriage. Braydon made the demand to unite the packs. Ours needed an alpha, his needed women. So my father agreed, and I did as well for the protection of my pack. Happy? You're bruised badly, but you heal miraculously. Wish we could figure out how to take your DNA and mix it into other women."

"You apply an ancient curse that forbids you from dying, add a Viking mutt, and throw it in a petri dish, and watch chaos ensue."

"You loved him at one time, did you not? Or is it true that you helped curse him?" she asked.

"I already told you that I did at one time. Does it make it easier to hate me by hearing it again? I loved him. I loved that fucking mutt so much that I didn't think about the consequences until we were discovered. He's on my soul, written in ink that cannot be erased. Do you still want to save me now?" I asked coldly, my eyes taking in the pain of hers.

"And I thought I had issues," she said, standing up to look down at me. "You are his true mate, Laura. I get it, and I understand it. If he chooses you, so be it. I have not fucked him, nor do I intend to while you are here. I won't be anyone's second choice. He has vowed to protect my pack in either case, and that is all I have wanted from him. However, I will not let you kill him. If you so much as try, I will make you my personal bitch."

I smiled coldly. "I never want to kill him." I stared up at her. "He goes mad the moment he falls in love with me. Better he hates me than love me, because it is the only thing preventing the curse from unraveling."

"Good, then we are agreed. You won't kill him, and I won't have to hunt you down and murder you."

"Not even close to agreeing. You think you'd fight

me if I had my magic?" I asked carefully, watching as the color drained from her face. "You know you couldn't," I snorted. "Did you know that a cursed witch need only release her light magic to accept the darkness in its place? I am both light and dark, and can choose the darkness to retrieve my magic. If they harm Hope, I will not hesitate to accept that evil into my soul to make those who have hurt her pay for it. Me, I can handle the pain. I can handle being knotted and having it ripped from my cunt," I hissed, knowing Braydon listened at the door. "There is nothing you can do if I reach for that ancient darkness, *nothing*. No magic, no weapon, nothing would be safe from me or what I would become. Keep that in mind, wolf, when you handle that girl. She has been sheltered and isn't a part of this mess. Her parents are coming, and they will rip apart this bayou to find their child."

"I'm not threatening Hope, Laura."

"But Braydon is, and he can hear me. I'll play whatever part he wants me to, but she is to be treated with care. She may be older than the lot of you, but she is a child in her world. I don't make threats I won't see through, nor do I ever give my word and fail. Thank you for being woman enough to care that I was hurt, but I can handle him. I've felt his abuse before, and I'm not afraid of it anymore. You see, I've come to expect it. I don't need your protection, nor do I want your pity. I am a witch. I am a fucking Cheveron witch," I said coldly with tears shining in my eyes. "I am no one's bitch, Moira."

CHAPTER ELEVEN

I waited undisturbed in the bedroom as water infused with lavender along with other herbs he placed into a large tub. Braydon lit candles around the room since there seemed to be no power this deep into the bayou, which was probably how they remained hidden. Night had fallen, and the darkness in the room called to me, beckoning me to the blissfulness of sleep.

I'd been almost there when he touched me. My body jerked away from his, and I crawled back on the bed, staring at him through wide eyes. He studied me as if he wasn't sure how to handle the mess he'd made.

"Your bath is ready," he uttered gently.

I didn't speak, glaring up at him in the house's silence, while the wind howled beyond the walls. Candles lit the room behind him, illuminating his immense frame. I felt tiny for the first time in centuries. Swallowing down the fear that tightened my throat, I removed the blankets, revealing the colorful bruises that he'd left with his vigorous virility. The flesh between my thighs ached with every move I made, reminding me of what he'd done. It took everything within me not to scream as I stood for the first time. Nausea swirled through my stomach, pushing against my throat as I closed my eyes.

"I can help you," he offered.

"I don't want you to touch me," I replied crisply with enough hate marring my words. He backed up as I opened my eyes, staring at him. "I don't need anything from you, Braydon. I want to leave here; do you hear me? I don't want to die, and I assure you, that is what will happen if I stay here. You say you don't want my blood on your hands, but you will have it. You already do, don't you?" I challenged.

"I will release you eventually, witch."

"No, you won't. Because you can't just erase that mark on your soul, mutt," I laughed. "You don't get it, do you? I have tried everything to be rid of it. I let them take my fucking soul to cleanse it, and it's still there. I have withstood rituals that tore me apart, shredded me from the inside out, and yet there you were. You are a part of me, and I am a part of you. Soulmates come once in a lifetime, and until our souls die, we're mated. End of fucking story. You think some backwoods witch can do what thousands of others couldn't? Good for you, keeping the hope alive." I walked past him, lifting the shirt to reveal more flesh that he'd hurt in his urgency to prevent us from mating.

At the tub, I turned toward him before climbing in to lean my head against the raised back. I ignored the bite of the steaming water and the pain as it scolded my most sensitive flesh as I washed his touch and scent from me. My eyes closed as I felt him taking in the damage.

"Stop staring at me, Viking," I mused as I sat up,

bringing my legs against my chest to stare over at him. "You've done worse, I assure you."

"How many times have you killed me?" he countered, surprising me.

"I didn't keep count," I replied honestly. "It's not like we have a scorecard. You are reborn after every death, and within fifty years of you coming back, you find me, and I kill you. Rinse and repeat. This is the first time you've ever found me early." I shrugged silently, leaning my head against my knees.

"Why did you love me in every life?" he continued.

"I don't know why I love you, only that I always end up falling for you. Maybe this time will prevent it, huh? Because I honestly don't like you at all," I laughed coldly. "In fact, you make me fucking sick."

"Is that so? Because you fucked me. You fucked me," he said, crossing his arms as his eyes burned with intense heat. "You came for me. You called out my name, and I felt your womb clenching me tighter. You say you can't have children, and yet I smell your heat. I felt your womb taking what I offered like it couldn't get me deep enough into it. You can mate, woman. I have felt nothing like it in my lifetime. You sucked me dry twice and begged for more. You think I'm fucking stupid? Is this a game to you?" he demanded as his eyes burned with anger as his hands clenched and unclenched.

"I am not whole, wolf. I cannot breed. I give you my word on it. My mother didn't want us to create life. You were an abomination to her. Created of the two things she hated most, Viking and werewolf. Vikings killed her lover, my father. Werewolves held my mother down and raped her for days, beating her while she was pregnant with me. My loving you was the worst crime I could have committed against her. Do you think she wouldn't include that into this curse? Her grandchild would be born of her traitorous whore of a daughter and her worst enemy. No, my mother was as evil as they came. She weaned on tales of the murderous invaders and the satiable wolves who both took from women. I killed my first werewolf before I ever bled my first monthly. I brought down thousands of Vikings before you, and had it not been for you, they may have become extinct, which I assure you she intended it to be."

"Then why did your cunt hold me within it? I think she intended for you to breed. I am an alpha, I have always been the alpha, haven't I?" he asked, and at my nod, he smirked. "And a true alpha, if killed with a child within his mate's womb, will come back to his mate in the form of their own child, so she has something to love and protect in his absence."

"What?" I asked, narrowing my eyes.

"What better way to punish you, Laura, than to make you kill our son and me?" he asked softly.

Tears slipped from my eyes to create small waves in the water I sat in. "We've never created a life, Braydon. It isn't from a lack of trying. We have worked together to prevent the curse from playing out. We worked as a team to find a cure to the curse, and when we discovered it was hopeless, you wanted to create life. You wanted to leave me a son to protect me. It didn't work. I am barren; everything says as much. Spells didn't change it, potions, curses. Nothing we tried worked, and every time you died, I was left alone to weep for you. You're wrong."

"Am I? I'm willing to bet that by the next moon phase, you're pregnant with my babe swelling in your womb."

"You'd have to have sex with me again to accomplish that, and after the last time, I'm good. Breaking my vagina is a hard limit for me, wolf," I said, standing up from the bath and reaching for the towel. He snapped it away and held it out of reach, watching me. "I'm not a damsel who needs her ass dried off, Braydon. Give me the towel."

"Fucking take it, little girl," he challenged. "You didn't wash your hair."

I blinked, turning back to look at the tub, only for him to heft me up and step into it fully dressed. My eyes widened as my mouth dropped open.

"You are mad, Viking!" I hissed.

"Not yet," he growled as he turned my body, so I was facing away from him. "I'm sorry for hurting you, but I know what to expect when a mate takes you into her womb. I'm not wrong, Laura. Your body held onto mine, and according to you, I've never knotted with you before, nor bit you. This time is different for both of us, is it not? A wolf only mates a female who is breeding to seal her womb to be sure a child is planted. If my wolf wasn't certain he could breed that womb, he wouldn't knot your tight cunt to seal it closed. I knotted you, and you held me there because you are my mate, little one." He wrapped his arm around my waist as the other reached for something outside the tub. He produced a mirror and held it in front of me. "Look at the bite."

I stared at the marks he'd left, both now scarred in the shape of a crescent moon. My eyes found his in the mirror and watched him as he stared at me before lowering his lips to kiss where he'd scarred me.

"You have my pack mark upon your flesh." He set the mirror back down and pulled me back against him as he settled into the tub, uncaring that he still wore his sweatpants. "You are an enigma to me. My wolf craves you, and if I'm being honest, so do I. That doesn't sit well with me, since your sole intent upon this earth is to murder me."

"You're wrong. My sole intent is to fall madly in love with you and then murder you. How easy it would be if not for the first part of it," I laughed darkly. "If I were to kill you right now, it wouldn't stick. I tried that too. I killed you the moment I found you one time; no emotions involved. Three days later, you found me again and caught me off guard with the madness I had tried to prevent in all its glory. You think I have half-assed this, don't you? I promise you this, wolf. I have considered everything except handing my soul to the darkness."

"What happens if you were to give in to the darkness?" he questioned.

"The darkness is the worst type of magic a witch can ever grab for. It is hatred and pure evil that consumes a witch whole, leaving nothing of her when it takes over. Once it has you, it doesn't let go. It promises you sweet things, but it is an empty void that is filled with those dark promises. I have tasted it, as has Avery. We are both light and dark, both immortal in a way, unnatural to our kind. It hovers in the shadows even now," I whispered, staring at where the shadows swayed with empty promises, lured by the threat to Moira earlier, hoping

I would accept it. "It wants us because we are endless and powerful. If it is freed within one of us, it will take thousands of witches to put us down. I can't reach for it without knowing it would slaughter everything and anyone in its path, including those I love. No one would be safe, and I'd have little control over it. There's a moment, a time right before it fully takes control of the host, where you keep awareness. A sliver of time that a host can change their mind and choose death instead of the darkness," I whispered hoarsely with tears rolling down my cheeks as he worried his thumb over my shoulder where he gripped me tightly.

"You can't just send it back from where it came?" he asked in a soft tone, filled with curiosity.

"Once it is called, only death can prevent it from entering the one who agreed to host it."

"And yet you said you would, to protect Hope from us with it? How could you do that if you allowed it to use your body?"

"I'd allow a thousand darkened souls within me to protect her, Braydon. She is special. She's also family, something I don't have a lot of. I trust three people in my life, and one of them is myself. I trust her and her mother. So yes, if it came to it, I'd damn my soul to hell to keep her safe at all cost. Immortality is an endless curse. I have watched everyone I love die. I have watched my bloodline die out around me without being able to save it. I have murdered the man I loved to survive, and yet he loathes me now for purely acting on instinct I cannot control. I am eternally cursed to endless darkness where I chose to love you, idiot am I not? I chose you, knowing what she would do to me if

I were caught, and yet I would still choose you because out of everyone I have ever known, you loved me when I was the monster that everyone feared."

CHAPTER TWELVE

Braydon

I held her body against mine as the herbs Moira gave her in the tonic entered her system. It was an asshole thing to do, using the trust Moira had gained with Laura against her. Her eyes grew heavy as her head bobbed against my chest. A chest she refused to take comfort from. I didn't blame her. I'd been a cold son of a bitch since the moment she laid her pretty emerald eyes upon me. She cannot love me before we've saved her. I've held secrets from her since the moment I met her, dark secrets she may never forgive.

I stood, lifting her tiny frame in my arms, uncaring of the water that sloshed over the floor. My home was much like the ones we'd lived in while waiting for the curse to strike us down. Little effort had been used to erect it, but then the home I built for her deeper in the bayou was immense and lavish, fit for the queen to my king. She mewled, making sweet noises that jerked my cock to attention.

Snorting, I replay the pain that flashed through her eyes as I'd called her perfect little tits anything but what they were. I'd made her hate me, but it was the only way to keep the curse from being triggered.

"Did you knot inside her womb as I instructed?" the old crone asked.

"I bit her twice, knotted her flesh, and then removed it as you instructed. She'll probably never wish to be fucked again," I growled, staring into ancient eyes. "If you had stuck around this shithole camp you chose for us, you'd know that, Mary."

"You asked me to help you; this is how you save the woman you love, lycan. I chose it for the leyline it stands on, but I have to move pieces around and push everything into place before that moon rises, and the veil is down. Now, focus. You are sure she has not sensed that you didn't die when she thought she killed you last time?"

"She assumes I am reborn," I muttered, placing Laura onto the bed before spreading her legs apart. My cock itched to fill her tight flesh. Her wet hair fanned out beneath her, the fiery strands striking against the crisp, clean white sheets. "She has no clue that I am hybrid, nor will she unless it aids to bring her to my bed. I see no point in spewing truths until I know if she will live or not."

I was a hybrid, born half-wolf, half-vampire, and turned berserker by countless battles that I'd survived. Unlike normal wolves, we are a stronger, faster, and more ruthless breed that couldn't be killed. To end the curse on my soul Laura's mother had placed, I'd given up the part of me that hurt her. I'd sacrificed the berserker within me to prevent it from raging against her body. It had hurt to part with that piece of me, but she was worth it. I had watched what I did to her time after time, never allowing her to know that I had witnessed the savagery in which it had attacked her tiny body. I'd kept my secrets of what I was, and who I was from her since the moment I met her, but with the curse being removed from me, and having enough time pass to be certain it was gone, it was time to heal the woman I loved.

"A powerful witch placed the curse," she shrugged. "I am powerful now, as I hold your female's magic, and the magic of the other Cheveron witches, thanks to Thea's hex."

"What are you doing?" I asked as she touched my woman's naked, exposed sex.

"Her pussy is cursed, as is the rest of her, Braydon. To remove one, we must remove all. I removed yours, didn't I?" she countered sternly.

"You made me go mad for an entire decade before it ended." It was better than going mad against Laura's body and abusing it as I had in the past, but it had felt like endless torture.

The problem was, if she loved me, and I didn't turn into the berserker, bad shit would happen. A curse had to have the pieces placed perfectly to play out. If those pieces were altered, it changed the game. You couldn't just end it without sacrificing something you loved, something that was special to you. She had to sacrifice something as well, and I wasn't sure she would be able to do it, considering what Mary had suggested Laura give as an offering to escape the curse.

"She can breed now," I pointed out.

"She always could, but you refused to knot her because you were afraid to hurt her, and your berserker couldn't, because he couldn't demand it of the wolf within you. You ripped your knot out of her in all its glory, and yet Laura survived. She is also evolving, unable to stop it as her true identity unravels. On the full moon, she will be as you are if everything goes smoothly. Pray to Hecate that she survives," she whispered as her fingers worked ancient runes over the pretty red curls that covered Laura's flesh. "You've been adding the tonic to her drinks as I ordered?" she asked.

"I have, and so far, she's drunk the tonic pure four times. The other times it has been added into her drinking water," I corrected. My eyes slid to the pink tips of her small breasts already hard and begging to be played with. "It doesn't seem to be accelerating her change as you said it would."

"That takes time. Continue giving it to her until she fights you to mate with your wolf. You can fuck her when I am finished saving her life," Mary announced with a pointed look at the tenting of my sweatpants. Her ancient eyes locked with mine as her fingers pushed through Laura's wet curls. "She needs it, and when I am finished, she'll be able to do it herself. She may not even want you to touch her, what with your ripping that knot free of this tight flesh. You did a number on her, wolf," she pointed out, noting the bruises that cover Laura's legs and cunt still a week later. "I'm guessing being away from her for the couple days only pissed your wolf off more, yes?"

"She attacked me, and my wolf sought to take her

down in the way they do. It took every ounce of strength I had to hold him back. He would have used me to rape her, to knot her without mercy to show her who the true alpha is."

"I'm guessing he also didn't like you removing that knot then, hmm?" she clucked her tongue using her fingers to draw patterns across Laura's navel.

"Knots aren't meant to come out until we finish mating. You said it had to be done to weaken her and start the process of her change," I snapped crossly. I'd wanted to leave it in the haven of her body offered. I'd wanted to fuck her until I was dripping from her cunt. The urge to cover every inch of her in my scent had been overwhelming, and instead of doing as instinct demanded, she started to bleed out right before my eyes.

"Even bled out, the curse within her is too strong," she exhaled. "Her wolf is so fucking buried within her; you may need to add more venom to your bite. A female lycan hates nothing more than to be pinned and claimed. Everything inside of her demands that her mate is strong enough to take her and make her want it. You are her alpha, so fuck her like it," she demanded, lifting her hand from Laura's flesh to sniff it. "Her pleasure is now her own again. Next, we will work on her soul. It's in tatters, probably from being forced to kill your sorry hide repeatedly. Show her some kindness, Braydon. She's known very little of it in her lifetime. You can see it by the way the darkness waits for her to reach for it. If I were you, I'd release that other little witch you are holding, and soon. Hope is a liability. Laura won't leave you; she's resigned to her death. Sadly, and rather unfortunate for you, she's ready to die. Her soul is tired, and it is in tatters. I will come again to work on her more. If she doesn't accept you, and her inner wolf doesn't awaken, we may lose her. Wake the bitch up; use your scent as even now she moves toward it."

"And if she loves me before you've finished helping her change speed up?" I asked softly.

"I said show her kindness," she snapped. "I didn't say make the wee thing fall for you. Besides, she may need a week alone to flick her pretty bean. I know if I had been cursed to just one male sexually, I'd be visiting every male from this side of the Mississippi to the shores of England and riding them twice. You must bite her again in the same places. This time, the poison need not spread within her as much. You must knot her flesh again, but Braydon, this time, leave it buried within her and let her know the pleasure that it can give," she explained, exhaling. "You must awaken her wolf if we are to win this fight. She is in there, somewhere. Find her; awaken the beast that slumbers inside your woman. There is no magic preventing her from becoming what she was born to be. You may breed her now if you wish. She should be in her first heat anytime now that the start of her lycan life has begun; without the magic to fight it, it is inevitable."

"You think she will want me to knot her? I fucking tore her apart to get it out as her womb clenched against me, fighting me. Her body sought to hold me within it, to take what it craved from me. I know full-bred wolves who have murdered their mates to keep a knot seated against their wombs. It is pure instinct, and they fight the male to keep it there. She told me to take it. That isn't something a female wolf would do, ever."

Her head tilted in thought before she shook it. "She should have fought you to keep it, and that's a problem. I needed her weakened for the herbs to work, but even weakened, she is strong. We need her hormones to spike, and her instincts to rise. If she doesn't transform, you will lose her forever. See that she craves your proud knot, wolf. You may also want to clean that mess up and add some of your scent to hers, so she's more willing to use you when she wakes. Then you can knot her and show her what it is to be truly knotted by a Lycan Alpha King. Stop being the weak Viking who pined for the pretty little witch's cunt and be the alpha you were raised to become. Bjorn selected you to hunt her down because he chose you to take his throne, act like it. Make it impossible for her not to want you, say your goodbyes. If she fights against the change, it only makes the chance of death more certain. I get that you don't enjoy being her villain, but a pissed-off wolf is better than a dead one."

I watched the old crone leave the room with the silver glow of Laura's magic filling her. My heavy stare dropped back to Laura's apex, the bane of my existence that drove me insane. I slipped onto the bed, scenting her need and groaned at her tiny hand that pushed through the slickness of her sex that I wanted to bury my face within and watch her come on it. My hand captured hers before it could continue, noting the red marks that glowered over her tiny pubic bone. My littlest witch would have been a runt had she been born into a wolf pack, and yet she was fucking fierce. Slowly, I lowered my mouth, kissing over the sore flesh from the runes that burned into the very fiber of her being.

She wanted me to knot this tiny witch after she'd told me to rip it out of her. The pain in Laura's scream as I ripped it free had torn me apart worse than it had her. Every instinct within me wanted to remain there, and yet we were forcing her change, something that was dangerous. I'd be fucking lucky if she ever willingly let me touch her. Not that she'd get the choice, because I wasn't going to fucking lose her again. I'd had to curse myself to this swamp to keep from tracking this pretty little she-demon down and claiming her. Every instinct within me had demanded I do so, and fuck if it hadn't made the wolf hunt faster and harder when I let him out and gave him free rein to find her. I'd found myself outside her little academy more than once, and had barely contained the need to take her.

I'd watched her praying to the stars, hearing her whispered thoughts through the mountains. She prayed I didn't find her, begging whoever listened to spare me death. She'd never asked them to help her, only me. Laura was a fucking hybrid witch, one of raw, unimaginable power, and she begged for my life, not hers. She had no idea of what she was or who her father had been. I kept those secrets from her, knowing that they would do us no good. I'd wanted to protect her from the pain that came from the truth.

My mouth lowered, hovering over the heat of her core silently. I ran my tongue through the deliciousness of her cunt, sucking against the soft, delicate flesh that I'd battered and bruised. I'd been a fucking dick to her since the moment I'd captured her, certain that if she hated me enough, we'd have more time. There was also the problem of me changing what she was, and she may never forgive that. She'd have to sacrifice something of herself to escape the curse, and I doubted it would be the one thing she's known. Magic was a crutch, something that had always driven her, protected her, and I'd had to strip it from her to save her. No, she would never choose lycan over magic.

She moaned, and my cock strained to reach her. The taste of her made both beasts within me rise and take notice. Pushing her legs apart, I cleaned the scent of Mary from her, wanting no one else upon her flesh. I'd almost snapped Moira's neck when her scent was on my woman. Laura was mine; the universe created her for me.

I'd known it since the first moment I caught her scent on the shores of England, watching her from a distance. She'd come to end me, but couldn't. The moment she looked into my eyes, our souls locked together. It was like finding home; knowing that she was created for me had changed everything. This tiny little witch who had come to kill me had me all but pining at her feet. I, a fucking berserker who could take down hordes of enemies, was brought to my knees by the most beautiful maiden this world had ever created. The best part about that was it had created her for me alone.

My head lifted at her sultry moan. My body moved to curl against hers, tracing my thumb over the tip of my cock to take the pre-come from it. I lifted it, pushing it against her full lips so she can taste it when the spell abated, and she woke from her slumber.

Gazing down, my fingers found her perky nipple and rolled it between my fingers. I'd called them tiny, unimpressive. I'd known she was listening, and I wanted her to think I didn't crave her. I'd called her tiny, too tiny, but then she was. She was my little witch, a spitfire that could bring a berserker to his fucking knees with the mere heat burning in her pretty emerald eyes. I'd challenged her on those shores and fallen in love the moment that sweet little smirk crossed her mouth at the audacity of my boldness. I'd wanted them wrapped around my cock, and worse, for the first time in my life, I'd wanted to taste a kiss. Not just any kiss, though, hers. I'd wanted to watch her belly swell with my child in it, and now she could have it if she chose to.

"I have loved you for a thousand years, and I will love you for a thousand more. If you hate me when this is through, then I will watch you walk away from me, sweetest heart," I growled hoarsely, my tone thick with emotion I'd kept hidden from her. "I pray to Odin that you love me enough to stay with me, little wolf. Stay with me, my heart. You're almost free, my love."

CHAPTER THIRTEEN

Laura

Something growled beside me in bed, waking me from a dead sleep. I turned over, gazing at Braydon, who growled again. My hand touched his chest, quieting his night terrors. His much larger one grabbed it, surprising me at the strength in which he held me to him. My eyes slid down his body, landing on his enlarged manhood. He was hugely endowed, rather gifted with it by Thor, according to him. I leaned over, laying my head against his chest to listen to his heart.

It was different than I remembered. Slowly, his heart beat through the twin chambers of his chest. He released my hand and groaned, lost in a nightmare. I almost snorted, hoping it was a painful one. Sliding my hand over his stomach, my gaze flickered to his, slowly continuing down to the thin trail of hair that started at his naval. Pushing my fingers through the blonde hair against the muscles in his abdomen, heat flashed through me. I exhaled a shaky breath as my hand skimmed over the silky skin of his cock.

A smarter woman would have stopped after knowing what it could do to her. I wasn't that woman. My hand wrapped around it, watching as my fingers failed to encase it. Licking my lips, I paused, tasting him on them. I moaned while another wave of heat rushed through my body. I released him, pulling back my hand, but Braydon captured it in a larger one and pushed it back to his cock. My eyes swung to his, finding liquid blue flames burning with need as they watched me.

"There was a bug on it?" I babbled.

"No, there wasn't," he replied huskily, sleep making his voice rough. "A saucy little witch was molesting me in my sleep."

"Was there?" I said, yanking my hand away from him. "Stupid witch is she," I muttered, moving away from him only to be caught. I yelped as he pushed me back onto the bed and rested his frame over mine.

"Not stupid, she's a curious little thing," he whispered.

His lips brushed against my collarbone, and I hissed, watching him as he slowly explored my body. Braydon's kiss left scorch marks in its wake until he found the curve of my breast, grabbing it with one hand as his mouth claimed the pink flesh of the nipple between his teeth, growling huskily as his eyes lifted to hold mine.

"What are you doing?" I asked breathlessly, pushing him away. My hands covered my breasts, and I hissed. Dropping my arms to my lap, I stared dumbfounded at my swollen nipples. My hand lifted, pinching one and then the other. "I felt that. I felt that!" I screamed, pushing my hand down my stomach to touch my slit, moaning as I did. "Braydon, I felt that too!" I announced, pushing my fingers into my sex as his heated gaze watched. "Ung!" I whimpered, withdrawing them. "Something is wrong," I groaned. "I haven't been able to feel my fingers touching myself since before I met you. Something is happening."

"Try again," he said, watching me through a heavy-lidded stare.

My fingers danced over my flesh while I spread my legs, leaning back to see myself better. I moaned as my legs started to close against the pressure my touch created. He watched my face before his gaze slid to where my hand was fanning my flesh. I groaned when his lips curved into a roguish smirk.

"This isn't good. It means someone is messing with the curse. My money is on you, mutt."

"And how would I do that?" he asked hesitantly, and yet I'd heard the catch in his tone.

"I don't know, but you can't break it, Braydon. I am…was powerful, and I couldn't unravel it. You do not understand how powerful and evil my mother was. Any time the curse is messed with, the darkness that followed her seeks me out. I am one of a handful of witches who can house it. It's already here because I whispered my willingness to use it against you, don't give it a reason to control me, wolf."

"You think you are the only one with something to lose?" he asked, skimming his fingers over my thigh.

"Don't touch me," I snapped, slapping his hand away. "Leave," I growled, crossing my arms over my chest, ignoring the razor-sharp nipples that argued my request.

"No," he snorted, laying back, which caused his cock to rise into the air.

My gaze dropped, my tongue slid over my dry lips, and I frowned as I bit into my full bottom lip. My mouth watered like that of a harpy finding a fisherman hanging over the edge of a ship too close to the water.

"Fine, don't touch," I warned, laying back to run my hands over my breasts. I turned, staring at him through eyes that watched him warily. It had been so long since I could even feel my touch that I wasn't sure how this worked anymore. My legs dropped open, and I leaned up on my arms, watching his brow hike as if he found my predicament curious.

"Need help, little witch?"

"No," I muttered as I dropped to the bed and turned away from him. "It's just been a while."

"Need help yet?" he asked after a few moments had passed while I stroked my flesh as he watched me.

"No," I growled, rolling my eyes to the ceiling. "You could turn away," I offered.

He chuckled, turning me over toward his hard body. His hand grabbed mine, and I jerked it back, but he refused to release it. I studied him carefully, watching him as he moved my hand between my legs and dropped his gaze to where he used my fingers to touch me.

"This is crazy," I muttered, noting that he was using my hand to stroke my clit. My body buzzed with need like I was seconds away from jumping him. "Something isn't right," I hissed, pulling my hand away and rolling from the bed. "I feel like a bitch in heat!"

His eyes widened at my words, and yet he just sat back, stroking his cock in a slow, leisurely movement.

My eyes locked onto it as I licked my lips again; groaning and forcing them away, I began to pace. What the hell was wrong with me? I was never the aggressor between us. He always seduced me with slow kisses and sinful looks that made my knees grow weak. Right now? Right now, Braydon looked like a bar of chocolate, and I felt like I had the worst case of PMS in the history of women. My body was hypersensitive, and arousal coated my thighs as if it was *leaking* out of me. I turned to make a pass at the foot of the bed as a wave of heat rushed through me. I moaned, bending at the waist to catch my breath.

I turned, staring at where his hand continued silently stroking his magnificent cock. The memory of it being ripped out of me pissed me off, and I bared my teeth at him.

"What. The. Actual. Fuck. Is. Happening?" I growled. "I'm growling!"

"So you are," he mused huskily. "It's fucking hot," he continued, watching me resume my pacing in front of him.

I scented the pearl of come as it left the tip of his cock. His thumb brushed it over the large tip, and a mewling noise left my lungs. Whatever the hell was happening to me, it wasn't right. Stepping closer to him, drawn by his scent, I paused, turning to continue pacing.

"Why am *I* acting like a wolf's mate? I mean, I get that you're a wolf, but I'm not. Human genetics with a little something added here and there, but no wolf. I know because, had I been born of your breed, my mother would have drowned me at birth and been done with me. My father wasn't a wolf, either." I turned, staring at him. "But you fucking bit me, didn't you?" I asked, with accusation lingering in my tone. "And the harvest moon of Samhain is rising. What day is it?" I asked carefully.

"You have two weeks before it becomes a full moon, little witch."

His eyes began to glow, and my head tilted; before I could stop myself, I was on the bed, slowly crawling to him. I shook my head hard, kneeling on the bed. My hand touched my sex, and a groan left my lungs loud and long. I wasn't just wet; I was soaked, and it wasn't stopping. My body was mimicking a wolf in heat, meaning it should drive the wolf nuts as he watched me with an amused expression.

"Braydon," I whispered huskily. "Tell me you didn't do this to me. Tell me you didn't make me into something I didn't ask to be." He watched me closely, working another bead of come over his cock. "You bastard, did you do this?" I growled through clenched teeth, fighting a wave of heat as moisture slipped free of my body. "How are you not mounting me?"

"Because I don't have to," he replied huskily while his eyes dipped to the mess between my thighs. "You're about to mount me and demand I fuck you. I will even be gentle if you want it that way. I wouldn't ever dream of leaving you in such a state of need, not with so many men outside the door just catching a whiff of your current predicament."

Pounding started, and I jumped, scooting closer to Braydon with wary eyes. "Are they trying to get inside?" I asked hesitantly, with panic tightening my throat.

"There's a bitch in heat in here, every wolf within

ninety-miles of here can smell that weeping cunt. You can come with whoever you want now, Laura. You don't have to choose me," he growled and spat out the words like they were poison. "But you have to choose someone. I can pick someone who can be gentle with you."

"You've gone mad, haven't you?" I whimpered, fighting the heat that built within me.

"No, but as the alpha of this pack, I promised every woman here that they'd have a choice in who they mated. You're here, and you get to choose, even if it isn't me." His jaw flexed with his words.

"I choose you." I didn't get the words past my lips before his hungry mouth slammed against them. His hand threaded through my hair, holding me there.

"Thank Odin, because I'd have ripped any male's heart out who touched my girl."

"Your girl?" I uttered, grabbing for his cock, stroking it before I pushed him back, watching as he leaned back slowly.

"Oh, my pretty witch, you were born to be mine."

I grabbed his cock, watching the glow of his eyes as it beckoned me to him. He'd changed, and yet my mind couldn't figure it out. I couldn't figure out anything; my entire focus was on the pearl-colored drop that escaped the head of his cock. My mouth lowered, lapping at the drop before I pushed the thick head into my mouth and growled around it.

"Fucking hell," he winced as my teeth scraped him gently.

I took more of him into my mouth, enjoying the fullness of him there. He brushed against the back of my throat, pushing my hair out of my face while he watched me. My emerald gaze locked with his ice-blue eyes. I started to pull back, only to force more into my throat as his mouth opened. A moan escaped him, followed by a growl as even more filled my throat. My tongue danced around the sensitive edge, swiping it seductively. Pulling away, I straddled his hips, brushing my fingers over the tattoos that covered his chest.

Leaning down, I slowly placed kisses over them until I found his nipple. His hands cradled my breasts, tracing his thumb over my nipples slowly, enticing me to continue my slow exploration of his body that I knew better than my own. His cock bobbed against my ass, and I let it for a moment before I reached back, positioning him at my entrance, then I slammed home on him. My mouth opened, and a moan escaped my throat, echoing off the walls. My body clenched around his, needing more from him. I groaned, staring down between our bodies where he stretched me.

"What do you want, sweet girl?" he asked seductively.

"I don't know," I said honestly. I slowly rocked my hips, knowing exactly what my body wanted, and yet it was filled with memories of pain.

"Yes, you do," he uttered, dropping his hands from my body to watch me. "I won't hurt you again, Laura."

"You always hurt me, Braydon. You can't help it," I whispered thickly.

He rolled me beneath him in a fluid motion. His hands pushed my legs apart, and he withdrew from my body. I whimpered from the loss of him within me. I was supposed to be preventing this. He'd been an asshole since the moment I clapped eyes on him. I wanted to tell him to go to hell, and yet my body was in absolute agony. I rolled my hips, beckoning him to me.

"Tell me what you want from me."

"Fuck me."

"I plan to, but I want you to ask me for what you need. Ask me, sweet girl."

"I can't," I growled, pushing him away to sit on the edge of the bed as another wave of heat tore through me. "I won't ask you to breed me. I'm not one of your wolves. I don't know what magic this is, but I'm stronger than that, asshole."

"We'll see," he chuckled, lying back on the bed to wait me out. "I'm right here and ready when you are, little one."

CHAPTER FOURTEEN

Braydon didn't stop rubbing his hand over his cock, and to make matters worse, I couldn't stop watching him. I'd paced for what felt like hours, snapping when he sat up or got too close. Everything within me demanded I give in or concede to a baser need that wasn't my own. It was like my magic was calling to me, beckoning me to him. Every time I took a step toward him, I'd take five steps back until I was at the wall again. I was a mess, with sweat coating my brow from the heat that hit in endless agonizing waves.

"Only you could fight this," he muttered, scrubbing the hand he wasn't using down his face.

"Go to hell," I snarled.

"Hell is watching you in pain while you fight something natural as breathing, Laura."

"There is nothing natural about a witch in a wolf's heat. That's what this is, and that is why my only focus is you fucking me. I'm not a mutt, Braydon. I'm a purebred witch. I'm like royalty, my blood is so pure. Pacing your bedroom with arousal running down my legs in a waterfall isn't natural! It's the opposite of natural. Damn, it burns!" I hissed as I bent over, groaning while the heat turned painful, throbbing between my thighs like a constant reminder that I needed him.

"You won't win," he shrugged. "You're a witch, but what else are you? You are the daughter of a powerful witch, but who was your father, Laura?"

"I don't remember him. He died before I was born."

"Your mother never mentioned him, did she? She never mentioned why he was killed by Vikings, or why she was brutalized by werewolves. Curious, is it not?"

"I have bigger issues right now than my father! He's been dead a very long time, and I don't think it fucking matters, does it?"

"It does. Vikings didn't kill your father. He didn't die, Laura. He left your mother because she was insane from the darkness she allowed to control her."

"You're an idiot if you think that is true. She hated Vikings because they murdered him."

"He *was* a Viking, Laura. He was a chieftain. He was the alpha of a hybrid wolf pack that invaded England by invitation of the king. Your mother met him on the shores and placed a spell on him. He lay with her night after night until that spell ran its course. He left her there, pregnant with you. He fled the whole of England to escape her, and she made it personal. She declared war on all Vikings. They stopped invading because of your mother alone. The king promised your father safe passage to come ashore, to rid England of the witches. She prevented that and slaughtered everyone who had come across the ocean with him. So they came back for her on his orders, raping her as she had raped Bjorn.

They brutalized her, but then she'd slaughtered their brothers and fathers, and Vikings are a bloodthirsty lot. She was heavy with child when they found her; she was pregnant with you. The daughter of a Viking chieftain and King Alpha to the Lycans of Norway. Did you think I was on that shore by chance when you met me? I came to do what they had failed to do."

"Did you bump your fucking head, Viking? If this is true, then why have I never heard it before? If it is true, why have you never just bitten me to claim me?"

"If I had known you were the daughter I sought when I met you, I would have. I'd have claimed you right fucking there on that shore before the gods, and I'd have made you mine. I didn't know it was you, and you assumed we'd been set upon by rabid werewolves. The children were tiny things that happened upon one of my men when the moon rose and had been bitten. I was born a hybrid wolf. As were you, you just never changed because the magic you held prevented the virus from spreading. You also never asked me what I was, so I never corrected you. By the time I had married you, I still didn't know who you truly were, and by then, I didn't fucking care. I was then chained to a wall and cursed; it cut time to figure things out short."

"You came to kill my mother and me?"

"I came to kill you," he stated through a sad smile. "I was sent to kill the child she stole because she couldn't be killed. Your father thought to weaken her with grief by murdering his own blood."

"You thought killing me would weaken her?" I snorted, exhaling slowly. The heat was vibrating through me, and my hair now dripped with sweat.

"Bjorn thought you meant something to her since she had worked so hard to take his seed and bring it to life."

"Then why didn't you try to kill me?" I demanded.

"Because the moment I looked into those pretty green eyes, my soul felt yours."

"I don't want to walk down memory lane with you," I whispered, dropping my gaze to the floor. "So my father was a hybrid werewolf, so what? I have never changed into one. I am one of the world's most powerful witches. I assure you, I am all witch, puppy."

"And yet that sweet cunt is dripping your heat because it needs to breed with my wolf. That's your slick, baby, giving me what I need for my wolf to knot that flesh."

"Because you bit me!"

"I activated the genes within your blood, woman. You don't need a full moon to turn into a werewolf, because like your father, you are not a normal wolf. You are fucking royalty. Why do you think an entire army returned for your mother? Because within her poisonous womb was the King of the Hybrids' alpha heir. You were supposed to die in that attack, not your mother. When he married and had another daughter, he tried for your life again. He had to be sure her seat upon his throne was secure. So I came for his daughter, his best and loyal berserker and assassin. What I found was you, and I lost the focus to find her. I found the other half of my fucking soul. I sent word back to him before we married that she'd been nullified. I sent him a locket of your hair as proof since he'd claimed his daughter was born of fiery red hair. The locket of hair you gave me to have with me when you went back to your mother, yeah, I sent his fucking daughter's hair back without even knowing it. You were the daughter I was sent to murder, which I figured out when your mother captured me with her spell."

"Why would you never tell me this?" I countered.

"Tell you what, Laura? That I was an assassin who came to kill you at your father's behest? That your mother took his seed by force, or that your father wanted you dead before you'd ever even breathed air into your lungs? That had your mother known you carried a mutated gene, she would have used you more than she already was? What would I have said? What could I have told you that wouldn't have given you more pain? You would have said I was insane."

"Maybe because that is insane!" I stared at him.

"You took my knot, Laura. If you were human, you'd have died when I took it from you. You survived my bite, and I was your cure. Do you have any idea how rare it is to survive either of those if your body wasn't created perfectly for mine? Your womb sucked me to it and fucking held me there. Not human nor witch wombs can do such a thing. You held me in your body. I had to fight to get out of your fucking cunt."

"Shut your fucking mouth!" I said while my knees hit the floor. Pain rocked through me while I held my stomach. My breathing was labored, coming in hard gasps as I fought what was happening to me. "I hate you!"

"Good, hold on to that thought," he muttered, turning over in bed, covering his head with the pillow. "Try to keep it down. I will need rest to handle you and your needs, little one."

I glared at him, standing up. My feet moved before I knew my intent, and then I was slapping him, scratching him while sobs exploded from me. He didn't hit me or hurt me. He did way worse than any of those things could have done. He pulled me close, holding me against him.

"You're a liar," I whispered.

"I'm a teller of unfortunate truths that are hard to hear. I have never lied about how you make me feel when we are together, or how I feel about you, Laura. I may mislead you, but sometimes it's for the greater good. I've known what and who you were forever. You didn't want to know, but I need you to know now and trust me, Laura. The longer you fight this, the worse the pain becomes. Let me ease your pain, sweet girl. I won't hurt you this time."

"If I let you do this, we could create life. What if that was her plan, to begin with?" I whispered through clenched teeth.

"Then she won't succeed. It doesn't matter. Nothing will matter if you let this kill you, and you can fight it. Others have tried to fight their first heat, and they died because of it. Why do you think we forbid female wolves to be out alone, unguarded close to their time?"

"Because your kind are possessive assholes," I snapped.

"Oh, I assure you that might have something to do with it, but there's also your slick. That sweet arousal slipping from your cunt, it's a dinner bell to my kind. It's a beacon to any unmated male that there's a female in need. They aren't gentle with them. They attack to subdue her, and most don't survive the mating. They can't help it because the wolf takes control, as mine did when you attacked me. He bit you to show you who the alpha was, and there was nothing I could do to stop it. Moira almost didn't, which was why I offered her sanctuary under the guise of a mating. She's wounded, taken down by a pack of males and one who tried to claim her as his mate. Her pack needed protection, and mine needed women."

"You're supposed to be her mate," I whispered hoarsely, watching as he pushed the hair away from my face.

"I have a mate," he replied gently. "I have a fiery redhead with the prettiest green eyes this world has ever created. She's tiny, but she's fucking fierce. She is what inspired Shakespeare to create that saying, and no one can say otherwise. You are mine, and you will always be mine as long as this world continues to spin on its axis. I made a promise to Moira to protect her, and so I have under the guise of being her mate, and yet I have never touched her beyond a kiss we shared to make you jealous. Moira used me for protection, and I allowed it. She doesn't want me, and I want you."

His lips touched mine, gently searching for permission. My hands threaded through his hair, holding him to me. Braydon gave, and I took, uncaring when he lifted me and pushed me down onto his cock. His mouth swallowed the hiss of pain before he began moving me up and down slowly. He pulled away, resting his forehead against mine.

"Tell me to breed you, woman. I need you to say it," he groaned.

"Do it, make the pain stop, Viking," I whispered,

slamming my mouth against his before I pulled away to cry out as he grew within me. He held me still, holding me there, straddling his legs.

"Good girl," he crooned, holding my hips firmly before he moved us, laying me back onto the bed as he adjusted himself between my legs. "When I swell within you, we won't be moving from this bed for at least twenty-four hours."

"That's a long time to be stuck that close to you, mutt," I whispered, grinding against him slowly.

He smirked roguishly before lowering his mouth to suck on one swollen nipple. His other hand pinched the other, forcing a gasp to explode from my lips. His cock slowly slipped from my body while he popped the nipple from between his lips, grazing over the flesh with his teeth.

"When I knot your greedy little cunt, you won't want me to leave it, sweet girl. I know you're insatiable, and such an avaricious little thing," he growled seductively as his tongue slid through the arousal he'd created. "Such a messy little thing, aren't you?" he purred between my legs, lifting his glowing blue eyes to lock with mine.

He used his fingers to trace through the silk folds, slapping it without warning. I cried out, dropping my legs apart while I lifted to watch him closer. It still ached from the last time he'd taken me, and yet I wanted him. My walls clenched with anticipation for his touch, for his cock to stretch me. Two fingers pushed into my body, and a cry of need slipped from my throat to echo through the room.

"You make the most beautiful music when you ache for me to wreck your cunt."

"You have a dirty mouth."

"You love my mouth, woman. You love what it can do to you, and ache to have it worshiping you, don't you?" he chuckled darkly before lowering his mouth to lick around his fingers as they spread me apart. "This pussy is soaking wet, little witch. You taste like the nectar of the gods. Odin himself would be pleased with the taste of your dripping cunt. Look at this mess," he ordered, watching me as I obeyed. He dropped his mouth, grazing my clit with his teeth before he sucked it into his mouth, moving his fingers in a seductive beat that had me teetering on the edge. "Give it to me, Laura. Come for me," he uttered huskily before he withdrew his fingers, devouring my flesh until my hands buried into his hair.

"Braydon," I warned, dancing on the edge of no return. My body spiraled toward the climax, coming undone as he lavished my core greedily. His hand lifted, squeezing my breast while the other pushed back into my body, filling it with his finger as he found my G-spot, working it over until I was screaming and riding an endless wave of pleasure. "Oh, my God!" I whimpered in shock as I felt my body releasing fluid, knowing it was to prepare me for him.

He sat up, staring down at my sweat-gleaming body. Settling between my legs, he watched me through glowing blue eyes. Braydon reached down, stroking his cock.

"Turn around, sweet girl. I want your ass in the air, and then I want you to spread your thighs apart for me. Show me what is mine," he hissed, raspy with wickedness clinging from every syllable.

I turned over slowly, lifting my ass as my hips spread for him. My back arched, and I turned, smirking at him while my lips parted to speak. "Think you're man enough, puppy?" I asked, watching as fire leaped into his gaze at the challenge.

"I'm about to fuck you for twenty-four hours, sweet Laura, you sure you want to taunt me?" he asked thickly. I swayed my ass in front of him. His hand smacked it, and I yelped, starting to turn toward him to slap him back, but he grabbed my thighs, picking me up by them. "I don't think so, little girl. You needed to be reminded who the alpha is in this room."

"I fully know who my alpha is, puppy. I'm just not sure he is up to the task at hand."

He entered me hard and without warning. My head snapped back while a scream ripped from my throat. His husky laughter echoed in the room, and my body gripped his. Muscles burned, my core sucked greedily against him as he pounded into my body deep and hard, without relenting. Braydon's hands held me in place, spread apart for him to fuck me while I helplessly allowed it.

"Fuck, you're so tight," he complained, lessening his movements. "I want to take hours just fucking you in every position, and yet this tight greedy cunt is milking me already."

I dropped my face to the bed, moaning as the orgasm slammed into me. Lights burst behind my eyes, and I moaned, coming undone as he pounded into me, prolonging the pleasure of the orgasm that ripped me apart. Deep, husky laughter sounded behind me as his hand threaded through my hair, yanking it backward.

"I didn't say this naughty pussy could come yet, did I?"

"Didn't ask," I whimpered, still locked into the never-ending pleasure he created within me.

"Such a bad girl, Laura, bad girls get spanked," he growled before his hand found my ass, slapping it before he soothed the heated flesh. My body tightened against his, jerking before it clenched against his cock. I pushed back, joining the fray with my assault on him. The hand that rubbed my ass slid to my hip as the other one directed me to my knees, held against his chest while he continued to rock his hips, plundering my depths. "A wise man once said, if she's savage enough to challenge you in bed, or give you hell, make her your forever girl."

"Mmm, doesn't sound smart to me. We tried that, got cursed, and it didn't work out well for us, Viking. Now pillage and plunder faster, or find me another who will," I said huskily.

His mouth brushed against my shoulder, and my breath hitched in my throat as his teeth sank into my flesh. I waited for the blinding pain to come, for the scream to rip from my lungs, but none of those things happened. Instead, I came hard against him. My body bucked, forcing his other hand to reach around my chest to hold my neck. His growl seemed to echo through me, holding me lost within the sea of bliss that it tossed me upon. Pressure increased against my throat, and his growl grew deeper, marked with possession.

Sweat dripped from my brow while he held me there, pinned on his cock as he marked me. His bite was erotic; the growl that vibrated through him seemed to reverberate within me until I was humming with it. He was claiming me, marking my body in a way only he could. I should have been fighting it, but everything within me wanted to be claimed. I wanted to be his, and I had since the first moment I'd watched him on the shores of my homeland.

"You keep gripping my cock that tightly, little witch, and you'll be knotted before I prepare you," he groaned, licking the wound. His nose brushed against my neck, and something sharp touched my throat. "Try not to come this time," he chuckled before he bit into my flesh. I exploded without warning. The first pull against my throat sent my body into a painful orgasm.

My moan turned into a mewling noise that was part pleasure, part wonder. In all the times we'd had sex, he'd never bitten me. He growled loudly, pulling away as something warm dripped down my throat. He licked at whatever it was and pushed me down, sliding his hand down my back until he touched against the arch.

"You are so beautiful," he admitted, and I felt him preparing to let loose on my core. I clenched around him, needing him to lose whatever control he had. "You are mine, forever and always."

"Forever and always, puppy," I whispered, grabbing the blankets as he began to move behind me. He wasn't gentle. He was savage. Braydon pushed my spine down, lifting my ass until he was buried within my body so deeply that it ached with every thrust. He jerked the moment my body clenched around his, the scream vibrating through me as I whimpered his name. The orgasm shook my body, creating a trembling that wouldn't cease while blackness swallowed my sight, and stars erupted in my vision.

"Fuck," he ground out and grew within me.

I felt him coming, felt the thickening of his cock while his knot sealed at the entrance to my womb. I moaned against the pleasure and pain it created, fighting panic and the need for it to grow more. Braydon was fighting it, trying to protect me from the pain. Growling, I slammed against him, turning to look at him with need shining in my vision.

"More," I demanded, moving to show him it wasn't enough. "Give me more, give me all of it."

"Woman," he warned.

"Stop being a pussy," I whispered huskily. "Fill me, wolf, I can take you."

He swallowed hard, turning me carefully until my leg rested against his shoulder as the other remained on the bed. He touched my flesh, forcing my eyes to where his fingers skimmed over where we were joined. He grew larger, rubbing his knuckles against my clitoris as he watched me closely. By the time he finished planting his knot within me, I was writhing against it, struck with a red-hot need to drain him.

"I should have knotted you the first time I took you," he growled, smiling as he lowered my leg and adjusted behind me, pulling me against him as he took me over the edge once more, following me there. I lay there, exhausted but in a constant state of hunger as if he couldn't sate the need to fill me fast enough. "Sleep, you will need it. I have no plans of leaving this pretty swollen flesh until it begs me to."

"I need more," I admitted with a blush spreading over my cheeks.

"You'll get more," he chuckled. "You won't leave

here until I have sated your needs, my hungry little wolf. Your body craves me, needing what it desires is natural. Your blush is cute, but when you leave this bed, you'll never blush again. Right now every instinct within you is demanding I breed you, that cunt is aching for it. Your womb is sucking me deeper, drinking me in. It will continue until this first cycle ends. You will be in a constant state of need, and you'll fuck me until I give you what you want, or it ends."

"That sounds exhausting," I muttered, fighting against the urge to uproot myself this time.

"Calm your heart; I have you. I won't let anyone or anything hurt you."

I closed my eyes, wondering at the irony of his words. He was the only one who could hurt me—or should have been. The hex had changed that, left me without magic and utterly defenseless against him. This Viking was the one man I'd ever loved, and the only thing I'd ever wanted in my entire lifetime. I'd searched countries, searched out witches who specialized in curses, and yet everyone had told me the same thing. It cannot be undone. Not without giving up everything I was, and even then, they wouldn't guarantee it would destroy the curse. If what he said was true, and my father was a werewolf, it made sense why my mother hunted them and the Vikings down. It explained the bitterness in which she'd hunted them; using me as a weapon against them was just par for the course. But did it change the curse? Nope. It just added more salt to the wound, since I wanted this life with him.

I wanted him with every piece of my soul. The problem was, I'd twisted it with magic, changing it to erase the curse that marked it, and I was sure of one thing. My mother had given us an out: through my death at his hands, this ended. He could go on, have a family, and live. He just couldn't do it with me.

CHAPTER FIFTEEN

I awoke alone, my body aching with every subtle move I made. I'd been knotted for thirty-six hours, which Braydon had been cocky about letting me know was my fault. He'd been stuck inside of me like some rutting beast, and I'd goaded him on. I'd melted the moment he'd growled while stuck within my body. The noises he made were music to my soul. I'd lifted to his touch, wiggling for more like some bitch in heat.

No longer able to ignore the proof of what I was becoming, he'd held me through the hysterical tears, smoothing my hair away from my face before placing gentle kisses over my brow. His low-rumbled growl set me at ease, and any time I started to become hysterical, all he had to do was make that noise in his chest, and I melted into him.

I fucking hated it. I fucking loved it, and worse yet, I was sure I was craving him already. He'd left the bed without a word the moment he'd been able to. Like he couldn't put enough distance between us fast enough. I rose from the bed, wincing before grabbing the clothes he'd left me. I was sticky, covered in the sweat of our bodies from the endless fuck-fest we'd just shared. Moving about the room was painful, and the moment I opened the door, I was stopped by a surly guard standing directly in my path. Green eyes slid over the sheer gown I wore, resting at the thin patch of red curls between my legs. Thickly covered tattooed arms folded, a sly smirk on his mouth.

"Welcome to the world, little wolf," he chuckled.

"I'm a witch," I said thickly.

"Yeah, and I'm a fucking fairy," he said huskily, shrugging broad shoulders.

My heart hammered against my chest as panic rose inside of me. He made a sound deep in his chest, and my head tilted slightly, listening to the soothing noise he made. It was wrong, off, not deep enough and not strong enough like Braydon's. A scream built in my throat while yet another wolf entered, growling to ease the panic that was steadily growing. I opened my mouth to scream, but a deep, soothing noise filled the house as Braydon moved through it, pushing me back into the room before closing the door behind us.

"You're not leaving the room yet," he snapped the moment the door closed behind him.

"I stink," I countered.

"You smell mated," he countered hoarsely. "You smell like me, your mate. Until you're fully changed, you're not safe from them trying to mount you. While I'd kill anyone who tried, I don't wish to kill my men, Laura."

"You expect me to stay in this room forever, don't you?" I asked through gritted teeth. "Like some fucking dirty little secret? I am not some weak-minded wolf who needs guarding. You don't get to lock me in a room and fuck me when you want to, mutt. I need sunshine, fresh air, and to bathe. I'm covered in sweat and your come."

"You're the one who kept demanding more," he pointed out. "I was fine with the first twenty-four hours being the end; you held me inside of you and wanted more. You're changing, and if you expect to live through it, you need to let me help you."

"What is the point of surviving it if you're going to go mad and kill me?"

"You don't love me, right?" he asked with a guarded look in his eyes.

"No, I don't," I muttered, but if I was honest with myself, I'd admit that he held me tightly while knotted deep within my core, he had broken down some of the walls I'd built against him in the last fifty years. "It doesn't change the facts, though, Braydon. The moment I fall in love with you, you will rut me until I am nothing, and you will kill me. I want to see Hope."

"Hope was freed this morning," he admitted. "She was spelled to forget you and taken to New Orleans, where her parents are searching for her. She'll be watched until we reunite her with them, and then the wolves will return here to tell me when it has happened."

"You freed her? She's gone?" I asked, hating how alone it made me feel.

"I just said that I did, didn't I?" he asked softly.

"So now it can end," I said through trembling lips.

"No, no, it isn't over for us. Now you become what you were born to be, what the magic within you prevented when it took precedence over your wolf. You will finish changing, and then we shall see if the curse ends."

It was cute that he believed he would outsmart my mother. He still thought there was some way out of this curse when, in reality, death was the only way. I'd been searching for the cure longer than he'd been alive, and yet it was almost endearing that he thought he could change me into something else and prevent the curse from triggering. I'd tried everything, some things I'd even tried a second time to be sure I hadn't missed it.

"I assure you, changing me into a horny ass werewolf will not make the curse vanish."

"Touch your swollen cunt and then tell me it isn't working. I'm not mad with the need to breed you, am I? I didn't die last time, Laura."

"You did, I burned you to ashes and spread them in the sea, Braydon. I sent you where I always do: to sea so you can return home to your wintery fjords which you loved so much. I watched your body burn to ash, which takes days. I stood there, sobbing hysterically while I said goodbye to you."

"Whispering how sorry you are to have given me this life. You beg Odin and my gods to spare me returning to your poisoned soul. You beg the Valkyries to claim me, your proud warrior lover. You beg Brigid to take me home to my land, to give me the one thing you can never give me. A child to love, a wife who will love me more than the air that fills her lungs, and the love of a woman who can love me without ending my life," he replied gently. "I know, I know exactly what you say to my gods. I heard you the last time, felt your pain as you screamed to your gods and goddesses that you concede defeat. To allow your soul to go with mine so that we can have whatever resemblance of peace monsters such as we can know in the eternal slumber," he growled.

My mouth opened and closed several times. "What did you do?" I demanded hesitantly.

"A witch found me and told me she could help us. She was your father's witch, Laura. Mary's only purpose is to protect your line, and you are the only one still alive with the royal line running through you. She has been watching and protecting over you while she worked on solving the curse since the day your father died. She found me when she was searching for you, scrying to locate what posed a danger to the woman she intended to save. I was what posed the most danger to you, and so she came for me. She offered me a deal: accept her help or die before I could ever find and hurt you. You are the last remaining heir to the lycan hybrids of Norway. I turned her away, and she cast a spell on me, holding me in a cell until she could explain what would happen.

"Imagine my utter shock when she described the young witch with perky tits, hair the color of the leaves in autumn and burning emerald eyes that I'd dreamt of since my cock stood up as a young boy. I heard her story after that. I listened to what I was destined to do to you in utter horror. I wanted nothing more than to be buried in the naked heat of your flesh, and she promised that I would. That I would wreck it until you couldn't take anymore, and then you would kill me to survive the monster I became. She told me that if I could withstand what she would do, that if I survived it, I could have you for a little while. She began the curse that would end the berserker once you ended my life. You didn't murder me that day, littlest witch; you buried the monster that was cursed to wage war against you. I no longer house him, because that part of my soul was sacrificed to remove the curse. I did go mad before you ended that part of me. I even went mad when she brought me back with her magic. I hunted you in the mountains of Washington in my wolf form.

"I sought you with a hunger that burned hotter than it ever had in my human form. I'd been born to be yours, as much as you were to be mine. I am and have always been hybrid. I endured the madness within the wolf, running wild for over a decade. Mary brought me back here, and I began to build an empire fit for a queen. Your people are outside this house, Laura. Those who endured the hardship to find you, to find the rightful hybrid queen who was promised them. I made them that promise and assured them that I would bring her to them. When you accept who you are, we will tell them who you truly are. I am cured, just as you are cured to be able to fuck whoever you want. Mary isn't some backwoods witch. She is older than you are, sweet girl. She is endless, and she is fucking brilliant. She also is aware of what we have to do to escape this curse your mother placed on us. Only one of us now carries that curse. It isn't me. I'm not trying to save myself, Laura. I'm trying to save you from your mother. As far as we know, as long as you don't fall in love with me, you're safe from triggering it."

"You're fucking mad!" I snapped, trying my best to absorb what he had been telling me. "It doesn't work like that. You can't mess with a curse and unravel it.

You have to find the way out. It has to be played out exactly as it was set. You saved yourself, but what is the cost? You don't play with magic; magic plays with you. It comes at a cost, Braydon. If you are cured, that means I am already dead. Don't you get it? My death is the price to undo the curse. My mother would have settled for nothing less. I betrayed her, broke her blackened heart with loving one man who was both things she hated most in this world. There is no way out of this that doesn't end in my death, of that you can be certain. If what you say is true, then good for you," I whispered thickly as my throat closed off with emotion. "I'm glad you are freed of it, but I will never be. Not until my death will I be free of my mother."

"You will die, and you will be reborn as a hybrid wolf, sweet girl. To become a hybrid, you have to die a mortal death. You are mortal, with no magic running through your veins. Your mother assumed you were only witch, never imagining that you were the two things she hated most on this earth. You are the daughter of a Viking, and Queen of the Lycans, Laura. You will die to become like me, forfeiting your life as a witch to evolve into something that can't be killed. You're my wife, the woman I have craved since the first moment I clapped eyes on the emerald fire that burned in yours. You just have to survive long enough for me to bring that little wolf to the surface, and she's coming. You took my knot and held it. You placed your teeth at my throat when I jerked against you, assuming I meant to withdraw it from you. You are more wolf than you think you are. I was born a hybrid, but you, you are forged from an ancient line that predates the first man. You were born with it pumping through your veins, but that magic that runs through you was much stronger than it was. I took your magic, and I awoke the wolf within you. Let it out, Laura. Let your wolf out to play with mine, and see what happens."

"You are insane, you realize that, right? I was born a witch, and I will die a witch. You think me someone I am not. I thought you knew who I was, Braydon. I thought you knew me inside and out, and yet here you are, thinking I am something I am not."

"You were at my throat when you thought I would remove my knot from your tight pussy, woman. That isn't something a witch would do. You lived through my bite, sweet girl. You took my knot, and yes, I removed it from you, but we expected you to fight me to keep it. Removing it started your change, making your wolf fight to come to the surface. That's why this time when I jerked against you, you fought me to keep it," he said as my entire head spun with every word he uttered. "I mated you a second time, and you did fight me to hold it in your body. You growl, and mine soothes and calms you. I'm not insane. This is our way out of your mother's curse. You can change; you change into the one thing she never planned on you becoming. You become your father's daughter. Become the one thing that was too strong for your mother to chase after or kill."

"Based on what, exactly? The fact that you think I can become this hybrid queen? I am the fucking queen, Braydon. I'm the queen to an entire coven who needs me. I need them. You're asking me to change everything I am and to become something else. Something I don't even know or understand how to be. That wasn't the deal. You were supposed to love me for who I am, who I was when you met me. You're saying you've plotted with this witch to change me into something else. You say you didn't die, but I watched you turn to fucking ashes! I mourned you, and you were what?" I snapped, throwing my arms up into the air. "Out fucking other women or agreeing to marry Moira," I asked through clenched teeth, hating saying it out loud.

"I saved her from being abused."

"And yet you abuse me?" I countered coldly. "Get out."

"No way, little witch. You're not just turning me down. I have fought for us. I have been forced to stay away from you so that I could be cured of the madness to protect you."

"You know, Braydon. I can forgive a lot of things. Abusing me without going mad isn't among them. Plotting to turn me into something I don't want to be is another. I loved you for you, never wishing to change anything about you. I *loved* you. You were worth enduring this curse for, even if it only ended in pain. Get out."

CHAPTER SIXTEEN

The heat of the bayou was endless. I had spent countless days inside the room, refusing to allow anyone in. I was in heat; that much was apparent. He'd started my change, knowing there would be no way to prevent it from happening. I wanted one thing and one thing only. *Him.* I wanted him buried within me, humming as I came around his massive cock. I wanted to taste him, to feel him as he took me to the endless precipice that only he could.

My fingers were a constant fixation to my flesh, slowly exploring it with the ability to feel it finally. I didn't even care when Braydon entered the room, watching me through heated eyes that grew hooded in lust. He wanted me, needed me as much as I needed his knot buried in my cunt. He didn't leave; he watched me while slowly stroking his cock. We did this for hours, me coming undone with my fingers while he viewed it. I wanted to weep every time he came, wasting the essence that I needed more than air. He wasted it, wiping it away with a cloth that I took from him, sniffing it as everything within me demanded I rub it against my flesh. It took everything inside of me, every ounce of fucking willpower I held not to do just that.

I had insane urges, urges that made no sense to the witch I had been. I knew they were instinct, that of a wolf in heat and not mine. My body was an endless ache; my pussy had a pulse. A pulse that throbbed relentlessly and grew more painful with every empty orgasm I gave myself. My skin was sensitive, making it easy to get off, and yet it didn't help alleviate the need that pounded through my cunt.

"I ache, Braydon," I whimpered on the fourth day of seclusion.

"Use me," he demanded roughly, his tone filling with pain as if he too ached from my denial to cave to the baser need that filled me. "You can't do this alone, little one. You're suffering needlessly. Let me soothe that ache, let me take away the pain."

"No," I growled thickly, the sound vibrating through my chest. "I am a witch!" I hissed like a beast as my body heated. Sweat caked my hair to my face and my body. My naked flesh was slick, arousal coating my sex from the endless touches and orgasms that I'd given myself.

"Get dressed," he snapped. "If you won't use me, you will find another to soothe that aching cunt. You will not suffer this alone. No woman should be left in her need to suffer, not when so many are willing to fix that itch that irritates."

He threw clothes at me, and I caught them, narrowing my eyes at him suspiciously. Braydon left the room, his shoulders taut with irritation. Slowly I slipped on the shorts and then the oversized top. I smiled through the strain I felt at being out in the fresh air. My body sang with the thought of sunshine.

I stepped out of the bedroom, letting my eyes adjust to the light. There were no wolves on guard, and the door was opened, leading outdoors. I moved quickly, wanting to get outside before Braydon sealed the door, or changed his mind. Emerging from the house, I tipped my sweat-drenched hair up, bathing my face in the sun's healing light.

Growls sounded around me. It forced me to take in the men that watched me hungrily. I searched for Braydon, finding him standing behind the men. He observed me, noting the unease the men's hungry growls made me feel. I was a bitch in heat surrounded by men who could fix that never-ending ache between my thighs.

Realizing what he'd done, anger fizzled to life within me. I didn't want anyone else. I wanted him. The thing about that was, he could fucking suffer right beside me for messing with what I was without asking me first.

My gaze settled on him before slowly turning toward the swamp he'd walked me through to get here. Hope wasn't here. Nothing was holding me to this place. They had returned her to Avery; she was safe now. I walked past the men who growled deeper, scenting the slick arousal that no amount of orgasms seemed to ease. Braydon's eyes filled with lust, pride, and cockiness as I ignored the other wolves.

My glare slid from his to the soothing pool of water that Moira had mentioned was their drinking water. I'd bathed in it unabashedly, and yet they were supposed to use it for drinking? *Disgusting.* Judging by the women who were carrying in jugs of water from a trail leading deeper into the bayou, I was guessing they'd had the same thought.

Slowly, I walked toward the pool, feeling the heavy stares of the men with every step I took away from them. Braydon didn't crowd me, nor did the others make a move to stop me walking to the water, where I slowly made my way to the edge, lifting my eyes to the open swamp that spread as far as the eye could see.

My body ached from the moment I sniffed the air. The scent of male arousal sent a wave of need pushing through me. Ignoring it, I reached down, cupping the water before I brought it up to wash my face. The cold water felt heavenly against my heated flesh. Standing, I turned to stare at Braydon, who hadn't moved, even though his naked chest coiled with tension. His tattoos drew the eye, trapping it in the endless strength that they offered. It took an effort to tear my eyes from his flesh, ignoring the need to attack him and take from him what I needed.

Men and women watched me warily. There were families here, couples that seemed immune to my current state of need. I wasn't sure how they were immune or up to date on my lycanthrope lore since other than Braydon, I hadn't wanted or cared about their history. Exhaling slowly, I faced the swamp. Braydon thought I would rip my clothes off and demand he take me, fool that he was.

He screamed the moment I started forward, running with everything I had left toward the swamp. Men snarled while women gasped, knowing that being in the middle of heat, a woman was helpless to do ought but lay on her back and please her alpha. Fuck that noise. I ignored the pain to my feet as I leaped over branches, propelled by the need to escape what I was becoming. I wasn't running from Braydon. I was running from what was happening to me. It was too much, too foreign in my mind to become something else.

I could hear his growl as he rushed after me; the sound of countless feet pounding against the bayou's mucky floor made me run faster. It took effort not to turn around and tackle Braydon and fuck him in front of the others, marking him as my alpha. I needed help and vodka. Lots of vodka to dull the need to bite him back, fuck, I wanted to bite him.

My lungs burned; my thighs quivered with the pain as adrenaline rushed through me. I rounded a formation of rocks, climbing it blindly as it tore the flesh of my fingers. On the ledge, someone grabbed me, and I growled, snapping until Avery's delicate features broke through the haze of lust and pain that vibrated palpably against my flesh.

"I have you, Laura," she said before Conner snorted, tearing my eyes from hers to him and his men who stared down at something below.

"Who the fuck did you piss off, Cheveron?" Mayhem asked, noting the pack of wolves who stared up at me from below.

"My mate," I shrugged nonchalantly before hugging Avery. "Hope?" I demanded.

"Safe and worried about you and back in control of her magic," she replied, gazing down at the men who watched us silently. "There's an entire pack of wolves chasing you, any particular reason why they would be?" she questioned, pushing her dark hair away from her face.

"I have doggie issues," I admitted. "I may or may not be…" Braydon growled low in his throat, and it caused everything within me to silence. My body jerked toward his, and I shook my head, dispelling the hold he had on me. "Do you remember my little soulmate issue?"

"I remember, Braydon, right?" she asked while her gaze swung to my man.

I growled at her, causing her eyes to widen as her mouth gaped open. "Laura, there's something wrong with your face."

"I said I have doggie issues!" I snapped thickly.

"Avery, step away from her for a moment, my love," Conner demanded softly, his dark eyes slowly taking in the way my head had lowered while my shoulders had moved back. "And don't look at the half-naked werewolf below. She's in heat; I can smell it on her."

"Laura is a witch; witches don't go into heat, Conner." Avery still stepped back, staring at me. Her gaze moved to the pack of wolves below, and I snarled without warning, snapping at her because her gaze had slid over Braydon.

"She was, yes," Conner admitted, keeping his hands up with his palms exposed, watching my every move. "We need to get her away from him because right now, everything inside of her is wrong. I'm guessing that nasty bite on her throat and neck has something to do with her doggie problems."

"You bit her?" Avery demanded, staring down at Braydon with hatred running through her.

Her magic whipped through the surrounding air, soothing the need within me. I reached for her, moaning with the need for the power. I touched her face absently, pulling her closer as tears streaked down my cheeks, longing to feel that rush of energy again, and she let me. She held me close, stroking my hair while I sobbed against her.

"Oh, Laura," she whispered, holding me while she stared at Conner over my head. I knew I looked pathetic, dirty, covered in sweat while sobbing against her because I couldn't get close enough to the magic that I longed to feel coursing through me. "Let's get her out of here."

"If you take her, she will die." Braydon's words rocked through me. "She's becoming what she was born to be."

"Her mother was a witch, mutt." Avery had no problem pissing off the men below. Growls sounded with her slur, and yet Braydon held still, holding his pack at ease.

"Yes, but her father was not."

"Vikings murdered her father," she challenged.

"Her *hybrid* father was King of the Hybrids of Norway. He escaped her mother's hold, leaving a child in her womb. Vikings didn't murder him; he was one. He was also a hybrid wolf, and that is why Laura's mother hunted both down relentlessly. I'm trying to save her life."

Avery paused, pushing the matted hair away from my face as she surveyed me. I knew my eyes were changing because everything was sharper, more focused. I could feel my gums aching, and the change lay there just below the surface.

A low, deep growling started again, and my gaze swung to the source. I lowered my head, sharpening my focus on Braydon before I lunged, leaping from the rock in a swift, solid, graceful movement. I paced around him, ignoring Avery, who gasped and tried to follow me.

"I wouldn't do that, waif. She's about to claim him, violently if I'm not mistaken," Conner chuckled huskily.

"The fuck, she's prowling like a bitch in heat," Mayhem hissed. "I want one."

"Little wolf," Braydon purred huskily, watching me walk in a circle around him while my nostrils flared, scenting him.

The surrounding men formed a protective circle to guard us against the vampire and witch that watched on from above. As if they thought we needed it. Braydon followed my movement, smirking as I slowly continued to walk around him.

"Oh, sweet girl," he crooned thickly, heat pooling in his pretty blue eyes. "I can smell your need. I'm right fucking here, take it. Take what you need," he offered, holding his arms out wide and yet he remained just out of my reach.

My hands balled into fists, clenching and releasing while I prowled around him. My body was a fire without an outlet, burning me from the inside out. My nipples hardened beneath the shirt, and before I could stop myself, I'd ripped it off because it offended and hurt my sensitive flesh. Ice-blue eyes dipped to my hard nipples before slowly coming back up to rest on my face. I didn't care that everyone here could see me, or scent my need that filled the surrounding area. My sole focus was the alpha before me. My mate. *Mine.*

I lunged, and he caught me easily. His mouth nipped against my throat even as he turned us back toward home. The wolves flanked us, not trusting the vampires and witch who followed us without invitation.

"Your kind isn't welcome here," one wolf sneered.

"I'm not leaving her again. She's my blood and my best friend," Avery argued as Conner and Mayhem flanked her. "I do not care what she becomes, but I do refuse to leave her again."

"Let them come," Braydon uttered through the flesh of my neck his teeth held, locking me into a sense of calmness with his teeth. His tongue brushed against my throat, and I growled loudly. My cunt contracted, and he growled as he was trying to get me back to the house to soothe my ache.

I scratched his flesh and enjoyed the hiss of pain that escaped past his teeth. He released my neck, adjusting me while he continued to walk us toward the compound.

"If you don't stop demanding I fuck you, we won't make it to the bed," he warned.

"I don't care," I hissed, pushing my hand into his pants while he did everything in his power to keep me upright. "Now!" I demanded, and he stopped.

"Take them to the compound," Braydon growled, pulling his cock free before he pushed me onto it. I screamed, crying out as everything inside of me clicked into place.

"Oh, wow," Avery snorted.

"Don't look," Conner countered. "She isn't your Laura right now. She's all wolf, orphan. You anger her, and she will attack. You look at her alpha, and she will do everything she can to murder you," Conner explained. He turned, staring at the wolf who had stepped close to them. "Show us where we can wait out their mating."

"This way," he said before pointing toward the barren swamp.

I watched them silently. A red haze covered my vision while I watched her move toward her mate. Once they were gone from sight, I lowered my gaze to the cock that was slowly moving within my core. My teeth sharpened with need, and I leaned over, licking Braydon's shoulder before I sunk my teeth into his flesh, enjoying the sharp moan that escaped him from my mating mark.

"Good girl," he purred before letting loose on me.

CHAPTER SEVENTEEN

Braydon carried me into the house with his arms around my naked torso, dressed only in shorts to cover my sex-swollen flesh. We'd spent hours in the bayou, ignoring the heat as we'd fucked violently. I'd claimed him, and he bore the proof of it on his shoulder and neck. He'd allowed it, encouraging me to ravage it to mark him mine in every way. I'd felt my body locking around his, holding him against the entrance to my womb, which had sucked greedily for his come to fill it. He'd given me everything he had, and when exhaustion had hit me hard, he'd growled low in his chest until my eyes grew heavy with the need to sleep.

Laying me in his bed, I watched him through heavy eyes. I wasn't stupid; I knew what it meant to have claimed him. Only a wolf can claim another. I'd bitten him deeply, and worse, I'd fed from his blood like a gluttonous bitch. He was weakened, and I'd done that to him. He'd swayed while walking me back to the house, catching himself and righting his steps.

I pushed my hair away from my neck, peering up at him in invitation. He watched me, a sad smile lifting his generous lips.

"I can find another to feed from, Laura. You need your strength."

I growled low in my throat, hating that he'd even consider feeding from another woman. Possession burned red-hot through me, and I snapped my teeth together hard. His glacier blue eyes rested on the exposed soft column of my throat. Fangs exploded from his gums, and I shivered without hiding it.

"You are mine," he whispered hoarsely. "I will fuck no other now that you are with me. I don't think you're ready to feed me though, little wolf. You are yet to finish your transformation."

"If you feed from anyone else, I will rip their fucking throat out," I hissed, and then winced from the murderous tone that had dripped from my lips. His brows tightened together on his forehead, and he kneeled before me. His hands smoothed my hair away from my face before his lips brushed against mine.

"Fine, but we may end up fucking again because everything inside of you is burning to carry my son in your fertile womb, sweet girl. Drinking blood is an intimate act, and there is no separating it from being so."

"And yet you would have fed from another?" I accused unable to stop the anger that burned through me at the idea of him with anyone else.

"To keep you strong and healthy, Laura, I'd do whatever it takes," he admitted, cradling my face between his hands. "From the moment I first saw you,

I have never wanted another woman. I have craved you and you alone since the first moment you allowed me to kiss you upon the shores of your homeland. I've loved you since the moment you slapped me for doing something so human that it melted the ice which encased your precious heart," he murmured before his mouth lowered, hovering over my throat. His fangs pushed through my flesh, causing heat to throb at my core.

"I love you, too, Viking." It was a whisper, barely audible against the pull of my blood. He backed up, staring at me with blood dripping from his lips. "I love you, and it doesn't stop, ever. I may not like you, but I never stop loving you. I'm leaving with Avery, Braydon. I will protect you from myself, even if doing so rips me apart."

He knelt back on his haunches, staring at me. "Leaving me won't stop it, Laura."

"Neither will me becoming something else, Braydon. You can't stop it from coming for us, and I am in love with you. I don't know when it started, but I feel it, just as I feel the curse starting to unfold. You may not be berserker, but you are hybrid. You can still shred me and murder me easily. It's easier this way. You have to let me go."

"You're my mate. My soulmate, but you're also the mate I chose to be my queen."

"I'm also mid-change, unable to use magic, and in the middle of a bayou with a curse that has surpassed every cure I have ever tried to stop it unfolding. I might as well be chained to a bed with my cunt bared for you to destroy, because I assure you, it will be what happens."

"Am I ravishing you? Am I hurting you?" he asked

gently, staring at me through beseeching eyes.

"Not yet, but why wait for it to happen? Do you want to have to be forced to murder me? I assure you, there's nothing that comes with the victory besides utter sorrow and pain. There's no adrenaline rush from the kill, only a sense of loss so deep and painful that you no longer care what befalls you. I never celebrated your death. I mourned you so many times I was sure it would lessen, and yet each time, I am bereaved with guilt and sadness so profoundly horrid that I don't wish to live without you. I don't want that for you. I want you to live, to have a life that fulfills you. I want you to experience fatherhood and know what it is like to be loved. You get none of that with me. You get the rush of falling in love, and the moment we start to fall, it turns dark and deadly."

"You are not asking me what I want, Laura Aria Cheveron. I want all that with you. I want babies with bright emerald eyes that glow with happiness as their mother's do. I want little redheaded girls who knock boys on their asses, who smile so fucking brightly from within that it's magic on its own. I want you. I want to live with you, to create a life with you. If it isn't with you, I don't fucking want it."

I sobbed and fell to my knees before him, kissing him as tears rolled down his cheeks with his anger at what we would once again be denied.

"You can't have me, because she will never allow you to. Don't you see it, Viking? The veil is coming down. Even without my magic, I can sense her here with us. You may have found a loophole from the curse, but she will stop us." I kissed him hard, holding onto him as giant sobs tore through me.

Knocking sounded at the door, and he stood, pulling me with him. Outside, the moon was full, and eeriness had settled over the wolves, witches, and vampires. In the middle of the yard sat an altar, a Samhain altar to the Goddess Hecate. Mary, who I guessed was Braydon's witch, stood in front of it, turning to stare at me in awe.

"Time is up, Braydon. They're here. She must choose who she is to become now."

"Wait, wait a fucking minute," Avery snapped harshly. "She was born a witch, and therefore cannot alter who she is. She is my family!" she cried.

"Does changing who and what she will become change any of that for you, Avery Cheveron?" Mary asked gently. "She will die without her magic, and yet now she is strong enough to choose her path. She can become hybrid and live through everything this world can throw at her. I have given her everything she needs to survive her mother's return."

"Laura, come with me," Avery demanded, extending her hand to me.

I looked beyond Avery to where the shadows danced invitingly. Ghosts stood at the barrier to the camp, among them my mother's wispy form. Emerald eyes that loathed with a deep hatred watched me, waiting for the last of the veil between worlds to drop. Her hair and dress soaked in the water from the river I'd cursed her to endlessly drown within sizzled as droplets rained from her to the earthen floor of the bayou.

"They're coming," I whispered, watching a silver-eyed male who stared at my mother intensely before his gaze turned, taking in my tiny form. He lifted his nose to the air as if he could smell the proof of my mating with Braydon and then tossed his head back, laughing loudly. He was huge, reaching seven feet in height easily. Powerful arms covered in runes and silver torques marked his royalty.

I didn't need a fortune teller to tell me who he was. The way my mother stared back at him with malice told me everything. My father was here; my parents were here to take me to hell with them.

"Run, Braydon," I whispered, the words barely audible above the blood pounding in my ears.

Avery turned, lifting her hands as lightning crashed down around us. Fires ignited in the shape of a pentagram, locking the dead out of the area we stood. Her wide, horrified eyes, held mine and yet the call of magic slithered through me. I turned, staring at the silver hue of Mary's aura; the familiarity of the magic she held beckoned to me.

"You can have it back once you have chosen your path, sweet girl," she crooned. "I have removed the curses against you, all but the one that marked your soul."

"Traitorous whore. You're nothing but a slut who breeds with a monster," my mother hissed, her voice echoing through the bayou in layers that shivered down my spine. Her eyes condemned me, and pain slithered around my heart as if she was crushing it.

"What does that make you then, mother?" I asked, watching her face contort with hatred. "You have lied to me for my entire life. I slaughtered your enemies without question, fed by your lies of what they would do to us. You told me the Vikings hunted us, and so must be slaughtered before they came inland, and I did. I slaughtered entire armies of them at your behest. I slaughtered wolves because you told me how they hurt you. My sweet mother, raped and brutalized by their hand, and to prevent them from breeding other witches, I slaughtered entire packs. The truth of it was, you fucked one. You, a Cheveron witch, had lain with one that you forced to be yours. You created me by breeding one, didn't you? I am not a traitor, nor have I ever been. I am witch, but I am so much more." My face transformed while she stared at me. My eyes turned into emerald fire as fangs clicked into place, sliding from my gums. Lines spread from my eyes as they darkened, glowing with what lay right beneath the surface: my wolf, my hybrid that ached to slaughter the woman who gave me life.

"You're an abomination!" she screamed.

"She's beautiful," the Viking countered hoarsely. "It must piss you off that the child you stole and kept hidden from me has now become what you tried to create when you took my seed, witch," he laughed coldly. "Part witch, part hybrid lycan," he mused through blue lips. His features were encrusted in ice, and yet he didn't look at me with hate or loathing. This strange creature that I'd never known looked at me through proud eyes.

"I will end you, Laura," my mother laughed coldly. "But first, I will take the one thing you crave most in this world from you." She tapped on the invisible barrier that Avery was holding in place, her features pinched with strain.

My eyes slid to Mary, needing the magic that she held to assist Avery in keeping the protective barrier in place. The problem was until the hex Thea had placed was ended, I couldn't get my magic back. I wasn't fully transformed into a hybrid yet either, which left me powerless to do anything to protect Braydon. Avery and Hope had figured out how to fix their end of the hex, but mine was still in play, leaving me magic less.

"Blood of my blood, I send you back from which you have come. Blood of my blood, I send you back from which you escaped, to the underworld below, to the depths of hell I send thee…" I uttered, feeling nothing stir within my soul. My gaze swung to Braydon's, and he nodded as if he knew what I would do.

The barrier hummed with the immense magic my mother wielded against it, and my throat closed with the reality of what was happening. Braydon had ended the curse, but only partially. He'd allowed her free passage from hell because of the thinning walls of Samhain. He'd unknowingly brought her right to us because the terms of the curse had been altered.

I couldn't save him without my magic, nor would I be able to defend him with being a hybrid. My mother was one of the strongest witches the world had ever created, and she was here now. She was a soul that couldn't be killed nor banished to the depths of hell by anyone but me. I had to send her back from where she had come, and I held no magic to do so.

"Avery," I whispered, knowing that she could hear me. "I love you; you're the best bitch anyone could have asked to be friends with. Tell Hope that I love her and that she will become the best Queen the Witches of the North have ever been ruled by. Braydon, my sweet Viking, I wish we had gotten our forever."

"Don't do it," he snapped thickly, his eyes promising everything would be okay, but they wouldn't be. "The barrier is holding," he urged.

"Live, live for both of us, my love. Have babies, pretty blue-eyed babies that you can love," I sobbed, turning to look away from him to where my mother's ghastly form stared at my mate, continuing to tap against the barrier. "I have loved you since the moment your eyes held mine, too. You are my soulmate and my world. I will love you from beyond, and death will not change that," I promised.

"You don't get to die, you little whore. You get to live! You carry my blood, my line. You will live, but this time he is coming with me!" she hissed.

"She's pregnant," Mary stated, her eyes glowing amber as she took in my middle. "Braydon, you need to get into the house, and you need to do it now. It's protected!" she screamed as the barrier shattered, and my mother rushed toward him with a singular purpose in her eyes.

"I agree," I whispered, accepting the darkness without hesitation.

"No!" Avery screamed, sensing what I'd just done. "Fuck!"

Evil magic slithered through me, contorting my body as the vile promises of retribution rocketed through my mind and heart.

"Blood of my blood, return to the depths of the river from which you've come. Blood of my blood, I banish thee from this world!" I shouted, causing lightning to crash against the ground. "I banish you back from which you came. I banish you from this plane. Hecate hear my call, and take this which back from where she came, hold her in the curse I of her bane, I banish you from this world, mother."

She wailed a blood-curdling shriek as dark creatures rose from the ground, grasping her dress. Emerald green eyes held my black ones. Her smile was victorious as she realized what I had done to protect the man I loved from her vile touch.

"I'll be waiting for you, daughter," she cackled.

"I won't be coming to hell with you, mother," I whispered, turning an apologetic, saddened smile to where Avery stood beside Braydon and Conner. "I am given, I am wed. I love you both," I cried as I lifted my hand, watching a dagger sail through the air before pain shot through me. Blood exploded from my lips. "I choose death," I whimpered, sensing the moment the darkness realized what I had done. Pain ripped through me, yanking my cells apart as the evilness of the shadows shrieked in denial at being unable to wield my vessel.

Braydon screamed, pushing the wolves that held him away from me as oily magic slipped free of my dying form. I hit the ground hard, jolting as it ripped apart my insides. It was trying to hold on to my soul, leeching against it as it began to leave my vessel. Blackness swam in my vision while I watched Braydon fighting to reach me.

Death wasn't the worst thing to come for me. Living without the man I loved, now that was a fate worse than anything else I could imagine. I felt Avery beside me, her hand covering the gaping hole in my chest as tears slipped from her eyes.

"You bitch! You promised you wouldn't leave me."

"I love you…too, Avery," I muttered as blood filled my throat, and my sight went dark.

CHAPTER EIGHTEEN

Braydon

I placed Laura on the bed; her blood coated my hands and body. Avery held her soul to her body while Mary held the bleeding from the dagger Laura had pushed through her own heart at bay.

"She's dying," Avery sobbed, fat tears sliding down a young face that bespoke of a lifetime of pain and anguish.

"She has to die," Mary explained.

"You're both crazy! Why would you ever want her to reach for the darkness? It is pure evil, and it ripped her apart trying to hold on! You killed her."

"It had to be that way to end the curse," I explained.

"You don't get to decide for her!" she screamed, her inner panic matching mine.

"No, she has to decide what she will become. She had to die to live her life without being controlled by her mother's curse, witch," I growled, unable to prevent it from escaping past the pain my wolf was in. Her vampire stepped closer, ready to defend his mate. "Laura shouldn't live in fear of me returning. I was spared from the curse by Mary, but Laura would have had to endure it for the rest of her time on this plane of existence. I allowed her to be hexed to remove her magic because it prevented her from turning into what she is. She is a purebred hybrid, much like the ghost who watched us from the corner."

"If she wanted to be a hybrid, then why did you have to chain her to this room? If she wanted you, why has she hidden from you with me? You cause her nothing but pain! Every fifty years, I watch her walk away from me, and when she returns, she is broken. Do you hear me? I have to watch her fight to even brush her fucking hair. She wishes for death after she takes your life."

"You think I want her to die? I have waited lifetimes to be able to love her. I have to live with that, knowing that once I do love her, and she loves me, she has to kill me. I did what I had to do to save her. And she was never chained, guarded at first to prevent her from leaving the room, but not chained."

"Does she look saved? She is dying!" Avery hissed through tears that choked her words. "You killed her, Braydon."

"She isn't dead yet," Mary snapped. "She is in between. She's hovering in this room, deciding which life she wants. Whatever she chooses, well, that is up to her. She is both witch and hybrid, but she will only emerge from death as one or another. She can no longer be both. Laura has to make a sacrifice, as Braydon did. He allowed his berserker to be sacrificed for her. Now she must make a sacrifice for him, to pay the cost to rid her soul of the curse."

"She shouldn't have to choose between him and magic. Its insanity and it will be like ripping her to pieces. You can't want that for her."

"No, I don't want that for her. She shouldn't have to choose, but that isn't our choice. She should have murdered me on that shore so long ago and lived. She chose me, Avery. She chose me, and by doing so, she accepted the curse. Do you know how she found you, witch? She felt the call of your blood, the familiarity of it when I was falling in love with her. She was pretending not to love me, and yet the curse had been triggered. I helped her clean your wounds. The oozing puss from the multitude of putrid bites that covered every fucking inch of your flesh," I hissed softly. "I sucked the poison out of each one of them and fed you my blood to heal it while she and I worked to save you. It took three weeks for the madness to slither over me that time. You slumbered through your nightmares as I raped her in the room beside yours. She never saw it as being raped, but I took it from her. I fucked her body until the life left her pretty green eyes. In berserker form, my only thought was to be deeper into the tightness her body offered. Cursed to fucking destroy her cunt, and anyplace else I would fit. Imagine loving someone so much that you would die for them. Then imagine seeing from inside your own mind as you rip them apart, fucking them in every way. She wouldn't do it, grasping onto whatever chance at a life she thought we could have. So you can hate me, witch, but I will never allow myself to hurt her again. I'd rather die than do that to her. I'm ending it, and if she leaves me, so fucking be it. She will live, and now she can be with whoever she wants to be with. Before, she couldn't have sex without me. Mary undid that curse because I asked her to do it. I want Laura to live, to experience life even if it is without me."

"But to stay with you, she has to choose between you and magic."

"No, she can choose whatever she wants. I'm letting her decide who she will become. If she chooses magic, she will remain as she was. If she becomes like me, that's her choice. Laura is strong of will and heart, and she burns brighter than any star in the universe. I'm giving her the power to choose what she wants to be. I'm giving her a second chance at life."

Laura

I heard them whispering, or at least I thought it was whispering. Darkness surrounded me, and yet there was a light just out of my grasp that I couldn't reach. Avery's magic held me here that much I could sense, but I wasn't alone. The silver-eyed hybrid who had sired me sat in the shadows, watching me.

"I am your father," he informed me as if he could hear my thoughts. "I assure you, in this realm, I can hear you, and I can feel you."

"You tried to have me murdered," I accused softly, uncertain if I blamed him for trying.

"Your mother intended to wield you against my family and me. I had little knowledge of what you were or what you would become. You were strong enough to kill my line should you have wished to do so. So I sent a berserker after you, intending to end the threat before it ever reached my shores. Imagine my surprise when my most fierce and loyal berserker did not carry out my order and instead fell in love with my daughter. I came there intending to carry out what he had failed to do and found you with him. You loved him blindly, without damning him for what he was. You didn't care that he carried the lycan gene, or that he was Viking. You loved him because he was gentle. So I left you there with him, alive. I make no apologies for what I am, or what I tried to do, girl. As a king, we have to make choices for the good of those we rule, and my sweet daughter wouldn't have lived if you'd come for her. Brigid was gentle and everything sweet. You were ruthless, and tales of you reached my shores, and while they made me proud, they also gave me worry. The Red Witch who slaughtered both Vikings and werewolves without prejudice. You slaughtered innocents without blinking. I assumed you were like the murderous bitch whose womb had grown you. I was wrong."

"You weren't; I would have come for you and your people, eventually. I am sure she intended me to. I love Braydon with my entire heart. That doesn't explain why you're still here."

"I've come to tell you that Mary was sent to find you at my behest. I want my line to live. You're the last one who holds my blood, and yet the magic within you is strong enough to hold the lycan virus at bay. You can choose, live as you have with your magic from your mother, or become like Braydon."

"Why can't I be both?" I asked.

"Because the magic within you will not allow it," he explained carefully. "The hybrid gene is a mutation. It's a virus that changes your genetic makeup. Your magic sees it and attacks it to heal you. You can never be both," he breathed slowly, watching me.

"If I choose magic, I lose the babe I created with Braydon, don't I?" I countered.

"Yes, the magic will attack him to protect his mother. He is of my line and is his father's child and yours. Unfortunately, you created him without magic inside of you. If you keep your magic, it will attack the lycan virus within you, and then your child. You will lose him, but Braydon will love you either way."

"I don't know how to live without magic," I admitted softly, letting my hand slide over the smooth stomach that didn't appear pregnant. "I am Queen of the Witches of the North, and I cannot rule them as a lycan."

"You are a queen by birth, Laura. Whatever you choose, I want happiness for you. She has cursed you for long enough, and even I tried to murder you. You've earned your time on this earth, so whatever you choose, I hope it brings you happiness. Now, for the real reason I am here. I want you to release your mother from the curse."

"No," I said without hesitation.

"Just listen to me before you ignore my request. I have waited a very long time to get my hands on her. I have made deals with the devil himself to get her. The only thing preventing me from having my revenge is you. You're so fucking powerful that not even the devil can pull her from that river for more than a few moments. I chose a realm in hell that is filled with lycan and Vikings who wish to play with her for eternity. You have my word, and that of the King of Hell, that she will never escape. Give me this, daughter. She took you from me, ruined your life and any chance of happiness you and Braydon could have, and she only drowns once a year in the river."

"She's supposed to drown for eternity," I grumbled.

"She does; once a year she's pushed beneath the cold waters until she drowns to death. It is repeated on the next Samhain, which prevents her from coming here, as she did this year. Something changed, though; my guess is it was you. Your magic was taken, and therefore she was able to come here. Consider it at least, for I fear her curse is coming undone with yours."

"Fine, but I'm going back now," I stated, regarding him carefully. I looked nothing like him, which probably saved my life. Had I looked like him, I doubt my mother would have allowed me to live long.

"So you are, I wonder, which will you choose, daughter?" he asked.

"I guess you'll just need to visit us on the next Samhain to see?" I smirked, turning to mist as I returned to my body.

CHAPTER NINETEEN

Beneath the blood-red moon, I saw the resignation in Braydon as he nodded solemnly. His Nordic blue eyes held mine before dropping to my stomach. He understood my choice, and though it was hard to stomach for both of us, he respected it. Tears swam in my eyes, blurring my vision as I watched Hope, Avery, and the others making their way to me.

"You're sure, little one? If you do this, we cannot undo it."

"I'm aware," I stated firmly.

Stepping away from him, I made my way to Hope and hugged her tightly. She allowed it, pulling away to stare at me before she too shook her head and tried to sway my choice.

"I don't want you to do this. Please, please don't do this. You can't ever undo it."

"I know what I am doing. I know the cost, and I can live with it." I reached up, wiping away the tears that rolled down her cheeks.

"If you change your mind, I will move mountains to

undo it. I swear this to you, Laura," Avery said solemnly. "I respect your choice, but that doesn't mean we have to like it."

"I choose my child," I said firmly. "To finish transforming into a lycan, I have to give the magic to someone else. I also owe a sacrifice to keep you and me safe from the curse, and this is what I have chosen. I prefer my magic to remain within our line. Hope will become queen someday soon. She will need the power I can no longer hold to rule. Her road will not be an easy one, considering she is what she is. If I thought I could keep both the babe and the magic, I would, but I know the magic that I love would murder the sweet son that grows within me. I choose the life that was stolen from me. I choose Braydon and our unborn son. I am given, and I have been since the first moment I met him. You cannot take my magic, Avery, as the unborn babe in your belly would be placed in jeopardy. Hope has her entire life ahead of her and loses nothing by accepting my magic."

Avery's hand cradled her tiny bump protectively. "Fine, but for the record, I don't like it. I prefer you to remain as you were created to be."

"Life dealt us shit hands, and yet we stacked the deck in our favor. We've been handed a second chance at happiness, Avery. I won't walk away from it now. I've never even allowed myself to consider having a child, and now one grows inside of me. You, you lived in the shadows of this world, hiding the damage that had been done to you. You are pregnant, and we get to be pregnant together. I'm only a phone call away, and you can visit whenever you want."

"It's far away," she uttered crossly. "You guys could always move to the mountains. It's actually safer up there. I don't like leaving you here, knowing you have no magic."

"You don't like leaving me here period," I returned, pulling her against me to hug her.

"That too," she whispered thickly, her emotions on overload.

"I love you, you know that. I'm never that far away from you." I said, smiling while I released her from the hug as Mary moved into the clearing.

It had only been a month since I'd come back to life, and while I enjoyed everyone being here, I wanted to be alone with Braydon. To get there, I had to end the question of who would receive my magic, or if I'd push it back into the leyline. Mary had agreed to hold the magic that had been released from the hex once I'd died. I had spent the last month in the arms of my soulmate, and we'd hardly left the bedroom during that time. Lately, I'd been eating non-stop, unable to ever feel full. I'd dealt with tears, emotional overload at the idea of being separated from Avery after being stuck to her side for so many years.

She had Conner, though, and was expecting their son, who would be born months before mine. They needed their space to learn each other again, as did Braydon and I. Plus, I couldn't stay off of him, and even though he no longer needed to knot me to satisfy my hunger, his cock was my addiction, and I craved him and it embarrassingly so.

I doubted that Avery or Conner wanted to hear us screaming in the next room. I know that I didn't want to listen to them going at it like teenagers, and if they were anything like we were, it's exactly what was going on in their mountain top mansion.

"I have asked the pack to move to Washington," Braydon stated, and I turned, staring at him.

"Without asking me?" I demanded.

"You are giving up the biggest part of you for me, little wolf," he murmured, kissing my brow before he pulled me close against him, letting his hand fall to rest on my abdomen. "Once our son is born, we will move to Washington to the mansion being built next to Avery's home."

"Yes!" Avery shouted, turning to look at Conner. "You knew, didn't you?"

Conner kissed her brow and nodded. "I knew, but I wanted to be sure Laura agreed with it before I told you. I have enough room for the pack to run, and your happiness is everything to me, waif."

"I love you," I said absently to Braydon, placing my hand over his.

"You guys are so mushy that it's sickening," Mayhem cringed.

"I want one," Hope announced.

"A baby?" Mayhem shouted, staring at Hope as if there was something wrong with her. "They shit everywhere, and don't even get me started on how much they eat. They scream for no reason other than to scream. Are you insane? Did the hex go to your brain?"

"A soulmate." She rolled her violet eyes and blushed. "I want love."

"Like your father will let that happen," he snorted, crossing his arms over his chest. "I doubt you're allowed to date at one thousand years old."

"Two thousand," Conner injected.

"She's old enough to date," Avery countered.

"You sure we should move next to them?" I whispered, smiling at the banter that had erupted at Hope's declaration of wanting love. My stomach rumbled, and Braydon patted it, watching my family arguing.

"You're hungry." His thumb traced over my flat belly. "I bet we could feed you before they even knew you were gone."

"Let's test that theory after I give Hope my magic. Mary is suffering from holding it, and we need her to be at her best since she's the in-house witch and midwife. Can't have her weakening when we are only on child one."

"Child one?" he countered before turning me in his arms, staring into my gaze.

"Oh, we're having a lot more."

"Maybe we should wait until after we have one before you decide to have more," he offered carefully. "You miss being knotted already?"

"Oh, sir, I think you forget yourself. I want you. I want the redheaded daughters and the life you wanted. I want it all."

"I can't believe you chose us over your magic," he uttered possessively, staring through guarded eyes.

"If I had to choose again, I'd still choose you. I want this, Braydon. Not because it's what you want, but because it is what I have always wanted with you. I was willing to let you go so you could know what this is like. I'm not that person, though. I hated saying it, and yet I would have died for you to have known this kind of love. It's a selfless love, and I don't even know his soul yet, but I love him so much it aches. We created life, and if I get to know this little life by giving a piece of me away, then I'll gladly give it."

"And if you regret this choice later?" he questioned.

"I won't," I said without hesitation. "I get to be a mother. I get to be your wife. From the first moment I met you, it's all I have ever wanted. I didn't just decide to give up magic, Braydon. I decided to live. You're my heart and soul, and without you, magic is empty. I've been powerful to protect myself, but I have you. You won't protect me because I need it, because I am still strong even without magic, but because I am yours," I exhaled, lifting on my toes to claim his lips. "I could only regret not giving life a chance. I want your babies. I want to wake up every morning and look into your wintery gaze and feel the heat that fills them. This is right; this is our story. We are rewriting it, and this is the perfect ending. If I had to write my story, this would be how I wanted it. I'm your wife, who is madly in love with you. I'm going to be the mother of your children, Braydon. Now kiss me, because I love you."

"You're my forever girl, little one," he uttered.

"You're damn right I am, Viking."

~The End~

ABOUT THE AUTHOR

Amelia lives in the great Pacific Northwest with her family. When not writing, she can be found on her author page, hanging out with fans, or dreaming up new twisting plots. She's an avid reader of everything paranormal romance.

Stalker links!

Facebook: https://www.facebook.com/authorameliahutchins
Website: http://amelia-hutchins.com/
Goodreads: https://www.goodreads.com/author/show/7092218.Amelia_Hutchins
Twitter: https://twitter.com/ameliaauthor
Pinterest: http://www.pinterest.com/ameliahutchins
Instagram: https://www.instagram.com/author.amelia.hutchins/
Facebook Author Group: https://goo.gl/BqpCVK

Printed in Great Britain
by Amazon